BAD! BAD! S.

By Glen Seeber

COPYRIGHT

This is a work of fiction. Similarities to real people, places, or events are entirely coincidental.

INTRODUCTION

Dogs bark. It's what they do. Sometimes you know what they're barking at — a squirrel, the neighbor's cat, the mailman, another barking dog down the street — but more times than not what set off their barking is a mystery you will never solve.

Fred is different. He's my dog. When something happens that upsets him, I have no doubt what it is that set him off. He tells me. That's right, my dog can talk.

And he's telling me there is something under the floor. Something dangerous. Something that needs to be addressed immediately. Something that isn't a squirrel or a cat or a mailman or the dog down the street.

My name, today anyway, is Carter. I'm a professional liar currently in witness protection. But I am not lying when I tell you there is a blood-sucking monster loose in the city.

My life is at risk if I draw attention to myself, and no one in authority here would believe me if I told them anyway, so the only ones who can stop this creature are Fred and me.

This is our story.

DEDICATION

To Topper, my best friend for 13 years. You spoke to me from inside the cage at the animal shelter. We didn't speak the same language but I understood you anyway. I miss you, buddy!

My guy, always and forever

Topper, 2006-2019

CHAPTER 1: SOMETHING

Fred made a sound, practically a growl.

I glanced up from the book I was reading. Fred stared at me from near the fireplace, his body so tense I could almost see him vibrating.

"What's up, Fred?" I asked.

"Sump'uh heah," he said, his long tongue working with lips and palate in an effort to form understandable words.

"'Something here'?" I asked. "Where?"

Fred looked down. I followed his gaze to the light brown carpet at his feet. Wall-to-wall carpeting, there when we moved in. New when we moved in, like the paint, the appliances, the plumbing, and everything smelled new except the old wood-frame house itself.

"What is it?" I asked. Fred had a limited vocabulary and I didn't know if he would be able to tell me, but it didn't hurt to try. He was good at getting meaning across, even if he couldn't pronounce every word clearly.

"Bad," he said. "Bad-bad!"

I went over to Fred and hunkered down beside the little guy. I could feel the heat radiating from his body. This was really upsetting him.

"Right here?"

"Yeh!" he said, then whined. "Nuh," then "Yeh," then "Nuh" again.

"OK, Fred, I get it. This bad thing is here, under us, but not right here, not right now."

Fred barked, jumped up and ran in a tight circle, his tail wildly wagging. He loved it when an attempt to communicate something really difficult was successful.

I ran my hands over the carpet, feeling for anything foreign or unusual. It may not have been a smart thing to do, I confess, considering Fred and I were in the U.S. Marshals Service's Witness Security Program. If someone had gotten a bomb into the house and set up a wire-thin trigger or hidden pressure plate to be tripped by an unwary footstep, for example, I could end up blowing my hands off, if not the entire house, doing this.

It wouldn't be the first bomb, either.

But that wasn't the kind of danger Fred sensed, I had no doubt. He would have been able to tell me about a bomb; this was different, the way a scorpion's stinger is different from plastic explosive attached to a trip wire.

He started to imitate me, I thought, then I realized he was digging, as if attempting to claw through the carpet and into the floor below.

"Whoa, Fred," I said, lightly touching his right front leg. He stopped digging. "It's deeper, isn't it? Down, under the floor, under the house."

He barked, spun around then stopped, facing me, and barked again.

On the nose, I thought. There's something under the house. Something dangerous, but not immediately so. Something Fred needed me to know about, that he couldn't take care of himself, something that wasn't a rat or a skunk or a neighbor's cat.

Something I'd need to investigate. Fred's instincts were primal.

I gave Fred a hug and a stroke down his back. He wasn't a big dog, but not a tiny one either. Come to think of it, I probably shouldn't describe him at all, since we were in hiding. If you must picture him, think of him as, say, a diminutive Jack Russell terrier mix. He isn't, but Jack Russells are cute and clever, and he's certainly as endearing, steadfast and loyal as any Jack Russell you may have known. Only much, much more intelligent.

As for what I look like, it's the same thing. If I described myself, and you saw me, you could turn me in for the reward. Just picture me at this point as, perhaps, your favorite actor in his 30s. Not too handsome, just average, and a little overweight. Soft around the middle, but not too soft. And in the early stages of growing a beard.

I finished petting Fred and got up off my knees. "Let's see what we can figure out, Fred. That thing won't stay hidden long now that we know about it."

"Yeh," he said. "Bad. Bad! Bad!"

CHAPTER 2: UNDER THE HOUSE

Fred and I went outside the wood frame house. It was painted white with medium-height shrubs in front, clearly built on a pier-and-beam foundation. That is, it wasn't on a concrete slab resting on the ground like more recent construction, but was held up several feet in the air on a cinder block foundation. Inside the foundation walls there were multiple columns holding up the floor — the piers on which the floor beams rested. Around the sides of the house, the cinder block wall hid the open space under the floor from public view.

Around the side of the house, we found a metal plate covering an access hole to the space under the house, the crawlspace.

The space between the ground and the floor joists was called a crawlspace because that's all it was: just space enough to crawl through. It provided access to plumbing and other utilities, and helped prevent moisture from forming in the wrong places and rotting the wood. Unfortunately, it also tended to provide access to termites, spiders, rats, skunks and anything else that might want to hide in a cool, dark spot and set up housekeeping.

I have known some who have dug holes under the floors of their homes where they could hide things like money, guns, other valuables and, as felt needed, bodies. As I said, Fred and I were in the Witness Security Program, and that was for a very good reason. A lot of people didn't want us talking to anyone and it would not hurt their consciences to see us dead, even at their own hands.

Now sometimes when there is a wood frame house built on pier and beam, a trap door in the floor may provide access to the crawlspace. But if this house had a trap door, it was well hidden by the wall-to-wall carpeting covering every floor except for the kitchen and bathroom. And I didn't think the U.S. Marshals Service would appreciate my ripping up carpeting to find one — if one even existed.

The other access to the crawlspace is usually outside in the back or on the side, where a hole has been left in the foundation wall and is covered by plywood or metal sheathing of some kind to keep the bigger varmints out. Like skunks, cats, dogs and, yes, children.

So it was that Fred and I crouched at an opening in the foundation wall, peering into the darkness of the crawlspace. The sky was overcast, spitting a thin drizzle, and there wasn't much light available from outside. I had a small flashlight. A penlight, I think they're called. AAA battery-powered, with a ring so you could keep it on your key chain.

Cool air flowed out of the crawlspace, smelling of damp soil, mold, mildew, old wood and something distasteful that I couldn't immediately identify.

Fred did not offer to go in first. A light drizzle didn't bother him, but whatever it was that he smelled under the house, that was a different matter altogether.

"That bad, Fred?"

"Yeh," he huffed, and without leaving his crouch he backed away from the opening.

Dogs usually like to go in first. When they know something is in there, it riles them up and they want to get at it and take care of things immediately.

Fred wasn't like other dogs. But you've probably figured that out already, considering he was talking to me.

Yet when I crawled in, he was there with me, at my side. Fred wasn't a coward. Fred was just prudent.

I waved away cobwebs, hoping they were unoccupied, and wiggled forward on my elbows and knees. I regretted not putting on a hat. I wondered if maybe I should have been wearing gloves. Fred stayed beside my hip. He sneezed, then whined.

I could smell it now, too. Something bad, beyond what you would normally expect in the crawlspace beneath a house built some 70, 80 years earlier, something like rotting meat. Like a pile of dead rats. Or a human corpse. *Don't think of zombies*, I told myself. *Too late!*

All I could see in the faint light of the flashlight was dark soil, more cobwebs, and of course the wooden floor overhead and the joists and the beams that kept this 80-ton house from collapsing on top of us. I made a mental note to get a more powerful flashlight; this one may have needed a fresher battery.

Then, in the deepest shadows in the farthest reaches of the gloomy crawlspace, near the fireplace support, I saw something move. Just a little. Eyes caught the light cast by the flashlight and reflected red, then were gone. It seemed like they were 2, maybe 3 inches apart, and I could tell they didn't belong to any rat, skunk, opossum or squirrel.

I felt a surge of hormones, as my body recognized danger and reacted to it even if my consciousness couldn't identify the source. *Fight or flight,* I told myself. In the crawlspace, in the dark. Now I was wishing I'd come armed with more than a flashlight. Body armor. Helmet with a face shield like the riot cops wear. Flamethrower. Well, maybe not that; this was, after all, a house built with wood.

"Fred," I whispered, "get out, now!"

I heard a scrabbling sound, and I knew he was no longer at my side. He barked, once, as soon as he was outside, so I'd know he had made it safely out.

I flashed the light around, trying to catch the mystery creature again, but it was no longer where it had been. Perhaps it was hiding, hunkered down in a low spot, or crouched behind a pier, or maybe it had even fled around Fred and me and was no longer under the house.

I hoped for the latter as I crawled the expanse of the crawlspace to where I thought I had seen it, then zig-zagged my way back toward the opening where I could see Fred waiting in the damp light.

It was no longer there, I decided, but while I was under the house I figured I might as well check the status of the pipes and electric conduits. Save myself another trip in the future, I hoped, if I was going to have to stay there for any real length of time. I found nothing amiss. No signs of rats or cats or elephants, and by now either the foul smell had dissipated or I had gotten used to it. The body adapts.

I emerged from the crawlspace into the dim drizzle and met Fred a short distance away from the opening. He was excited to see me, jumping around and licking my face as I moved from the shadow into the daylight, as if I'd been gone forever.

I hugged him again and together we looked into the darkness under the house. "Still there?" I asked.

He crept up to the opening and held real still. While it appeared as if he was just staring into the darkness, I knew his other senses were what were really hard at work, listening and smelling, so I held motionless and said nothing.

Fred sneezed again, then said, "Nuh. Emp'y."

"Good," I said, and he backed away while I wrestled the metal covering back over the hole in the foundation wall.

CHAPTER 3: ESCAPE ROUTE

Back inside the house, I cleaned dirt off Fred's paws, then I showered, double-shampooing my hair to be sure nothing creepy-crawly was nesting in it, and changed clothes. Afterward I sat on the floor with Fred in front of the fireplace, where he had issued the initial warning.

"Any change?"

"Nuh," he huffed.

Whatever it was, was gone.

"Any idea what it was?" I asked. He probably couldn't tell me, but it didn't hurt to ask.

"Nuh. Bad. Bad-bad."

"Gotcha," I said.

The face of the fireplace was built with native stone. It looked like each piece was hand-selected to fit next to the pieces surrounding it, like a large 3-D jigsaw puzzle made of stone. A lot of workmanship had gone into that fireplace, back in the day when workmanship was prized and praiseworthy. The rest of the house was OK, but the fireplace was what made the house worth staying in.

And through the years, no one had painted it. Points for that.

The mantel was a rectangular slab of the same stone. Any Christmas stockings would have to be taped to it, or else weighed down by something resting on top of the mantel. I didn't expect that to happen at any time while I still lived here, but one never knows. Above the mantel was a large painting of a seascape with a tiny white-sailed sailboat almost lost in the blue-green waves that looked like it might have been bought in a surplus-equipment sale from a hotel facing bankruptcy.

Then again, it could have been acquired from a drug dealer in an asset confiscation move by the federal government. I wasn't curious enough to ask.

The firebox was deep and blackened by countless log fires through the decades. A pair of andirons — a sort of metal cradle — held four logs, waiting for their turn to be set alight — but that wouldn't happen for a long time, since the weather outside was mild now. They were there for show, basically, because an empty fireplace is just a dark hole in the wall. A decorative fireplace screen, made with a metal scrollwork backed by a heavy iron mesh, separated the firebox from the room, and no doubt served to keep sparks from flying out and setting everything on fire.

And this fireplace had a secret beneath it that Fred had discovered.

I lay down on the floor, gazing up at the fireplace, and Fred snuggled up between my arm and side, resting his head on my shoulder, watching my face as I thought.

"When I first smelled it, whatever it was," I told him, "the thing that came to mind was a body buried under the house."

"Yeh," he huffed. We'd had experience with that, and it wasn't something that was easy to put out of mind. Then: "Nuh."

"You're right, Fred. First impressions aside, it wasn't a body. It was something alive. I saw it move. I saw its eyes, just for a moment, then it was gone."

"Yeh."

"You saw it, too?"

"Yeh."

"After I told you to get out, did you notice it get in front of you and leave first?"

"Nuh," Fred said.

"And you would have noticed if it had come out behind you."

"Yeh."

"So if it didn't get out first, and it didn't slip out between the time you left and the time I left, then it must still be under the house," I said.

"Nuh," he said. "Nuh heah."

"Gone-gone, huh?"

"Yeh."

"Then there's another way to get in and out."

"Yeh," he said.

"Let's go find it."

The drizzle had let up and the clouds were parting overhead, bringing sunlight and a freshness to the day that hadn't been there earlier. Off in the distance I heard a lawnmower as someone refused to allow the damp grass to stop them.

We circled the house, Fred sniffing the ground as I checked the foundation wall for openings. I found the usual vents, which allowed the crawlspace to breathe so that moisture did not build up inside, but they were screened over so that only something small could slip through. Like ants, termites, really skinny mice.

Fred stopped beside the chimney, then backed away, sneezing again.

Unlike the fireplace inside, the chimney was not made of native stone pieced together. Instead, it was built with bricks and mortar.

At the base of the bricks was a metal plate on a hinge, allowing outside access to an ash dump at the rear of the firebox, where ashes could be pushed from the inside to be removed later on from the outside. Although the plate was closed, I saw ashes on the ground, indicating something had come out through the ... umm ... ash hole.

I pulled the plate open and found it was spring-loaded, ready to snap closed again when released. I switched on the flashlight and looked inside. There was the ash dump, as expected, but to one side of the pit I found an opening that gave access to and from the crawlspace.

This meant whatever that thing Fred noticed was, it could have come into the house, with us, any time it wanted to, merely by passing through the firebox.

In the back yard, a charcoal grill had been made with cinder blocks, apparently built by or for a previous occupant. Inside the garage were some cinder blocks that I was guessing had been left over. They weren't as cosmetically perfect as the ones in the grill, which is probably why they were surplus, but I didn't mind using them to block the access panel on the chimney so it would be impossible for the average critter to get back in that way.

I made a mental note to see about plugging that hole between the ash dump and the crawlspace and about finding some way to put a lock on the access panel so it could be opened only when it was time to remove ashes.

Meanwhile, Fred returned from following his nose to the back fence. "Nuh heah," he said.

"Out the back way and through the fence somehow?"

"Yeh."

"OK. I guess that takes care of that."

He didn't respond. Sometimes I think Fred may be smarter than me.

CHAPTER 4: BAD DREAMS

I didn't sleep well that night. Neither did Fred.

I dreamed of those eyes in the shadows of the crawlspace, that this time they didn't just close against the light and go away, but instead came closer and closer to me as I lay, paralyzed, trapped under 80 tons of house. A feeling of dread swept over me, followed by terror, and I struggled to move but was held in place by the cobwebs I'd waved my way through earlier.

I felt a hot, foul-smelling breath on my face, then something in the darkness licked my throat and I jerked awake.

"Fred?" I said. I could feel him down by my side, on top of the covers. He was whining and seemed to be struggling, almost as if his dreams were as disturbing as mine.

I stroked his back and scratched between his ears. "It's OK, Fred," I said, softly. "Just a bad dream."

He settled down and his breathing returned to normal, and my thoughts turned to my own nightmare.

I touched my throat where I'd felt the lick: It was dry and scratchy with beard stubble.

"Just a bad dream," I repeated, this time for my own benefit, and I adjusted the pillow, turned slightly to be more on my side without disturbing Fred, and closed my eyes to try to sleep again.

They wouldn't stay closed.

I switched on the lamp beside the bed and in its cool yellow glow I scanned the bedroom for anything out of place. Fred continued to sleep, and I edged out of bed carefully so as not to disturb him, then for the first time longer than I could remember checked under the bed, behind the closet door and then the hallway outside the bedroom.

Then, for good measure, I emptied my bladder in the bathroom, fixed myself a small sandwich and glass of milk in the kitchen, and checked the locks on all the doors and windows, confirmed that there were no ashes indicating tracks leading into the house from the fireplace, and went on to check every other room as well.

I was halfway through the search when I realized Fred was following me, doing pretty much the same thing. I gave him part of my sandwich.

We checked the closet and under the bed together before finally both crawling under the covers and closing our eyes to sleep.

"Everything OK, Fred?"

"Yeh."

It was slow in coming, but we both finally drifted off.

CHAPTER 5: U.S. MARSHAL

The next day, I called U.S. Marshal Penny Ransome, partly to let her know what was going on, and partly because I wanted to hear her voice. After all, other than Fred, she was the only friend I had left. At least, the only one I could talk to without fear of betrayal.

She's a short, solid woman of African ancestry with a serious demeanor and a reluctance for chitchat. She seldom smiles, but when she does, it's like the sun suddenly coming out on a gloomy day.

She knew about Fred, which was a good thing. I don't talk to others about Fred talking to me, partly because people would look at me as if I'm crazy. Penny was that way at first, too, but that was before Fred decided he trusted her enough to talk to her.

That was also before I realized he wouldn't talk to just anyone. It had to be his decision, not mine. Lesson learned.

"Is this really worth a call to the U.S. Marshals Service?" Penny asked. Fred's ears perked up as he recognized her voice. I had her on speaker.

"Other than Fred, you're the closest thing I've got to a friend right now, Penny," I said. "You know, Witness Security Program ..."

She sighed. "I know that, Carter."

"I gave up my life, my career, my family, my friends, my home ..."

"Your career came to a screeching halt, Carter, your friends disowned you, your family all want to kill you and your home was a smoking crater in the ground when you last saw it," she reminded me, as she does every time the conversation turns to this topic. "I'm not calling you a liar — after all, you're our star witness — but you do have a tendency to stretch the truth."

Fred was wagging his tail, and a wide grin spread across his face. I winked at him.

"So, as I said," I said, ignoring her dig at my character, "besides Fred, you're the closest thing I have to a friend."

"Huh!" she said. I ignored her.

"Until this beard grows out more, you've made it clear you don't want me going out in public where I might be recognized, so my prospects of making more friends are fairly limited at the moment."

She sighed again. "Really, Carter ..."

"Besides, Penny, I really like you."

I could tell she smiled at this. It's amazing how sometimes you can pick up on the sound of muscle contractions over the telephone.

"I like you, too, Carter," she said slowly, begrudgingly, as if it caused physical pain to say it. Then, in a normal tone of voice, "So what's really going on?"

"I don't know, exactly, but it's got Fred bothered, and that bothers me."

"Hmm," she said, and paused. I could tell she was thinking: *Do I really want to hear this?* "OK, tell me what happened."

I described Fred's reaction to the bad thing under the floor, then our expedition through the crawlspace and the strange eyes that appeared then disappeared in the shadows. The smell, and the dreams.

"Did you have the same dream, Fred?" Penny asked.

"Yeh."

"Well, I'm not a psychologist," she said, "but I know that traumatic experiences such as what you've had don't just go away when they're over with. The effects can linger for months, even years, and come back to haunt you at any time. They can be triggered by the most innocuous of things, like a smell, a few notes from a song, the glimpse of a color ..."

"Or eyes reflecting a flashlight from the shadows of a crawlspace," I said.

"Exactly," she said.

"Nuh," Fred said.

"What's that?" Penny asked.

"Fred disagrees. And, frankly, I do, too."

"No, seriously, this is a real thing," Penny said. "I've seen it with other people."

"I know that. It's just that Fred and I don't think this is a trigger response to recent trauma. Something else is going on. We just don't know for certain what it is."

"So what do you want me to do about it? I can't launch a full-scale U.S. Marshals Service investigation into some strange creature under your floor, and have it turn out to be a rabid raccoon or whatever. We have bigger things to deal with."

I looked at Fred and he stared back at me. Perhaps I'd been the boy who cried "Wolf!" too many times already. As I recall the story, eventually the townsfolk ignore the boy's cries of warning, and the wolf gets him and all of the sheep as well. Time to show Penny that this was no wolf. Or, at least, not a rabid raccoon.

"I'm sure I can handle it if it's a 'rabid raccoon,'" I said. "I just thought you might want to add a note to my file about this, in case it turns out to be bigger than a raccoon."

"Well, whatever you do, try to avoid publicity. Even with your beard and your new hair color — you did dye it, right?"

"I did. My beard is growing in red naturally, so I've only had to tint my hair to match."

"OK, then, even with those changes, you don't want to call any undue notice to yourself until we get everything and everyone locked down from this end. And not even then, really. So, never. Avoid publicity, whatever you do."

"Gotcha," I said. "I'll cancel my interview with the editorial board this afternoon and see if I can get out of doing the photo spread in GQ."

She caught a chuckle and strangled it with the ease of government training. "'GQ,' really," she said. "Goodbye, Carter."

"Goodbye, Penny."

"Pye," Fred said.

I looked at him, wondering how he was able to pronounce "bad" so clearly, but when he tried to say "bye" it came out more like he was asking for "pie." Then again, he was a dog. Perhaps he was asking for pie, and it just happened that we had some in the fridge.

"Hey, Fred, you want some pie?"

"Yeh!"

CHAPTER 6: NEIGHBORS

Several days went by without incident. My beard grew some more and it didn't itch as bad as it had at first. I snapped the leash to Fred's thick leather collar — one he'd chosen for himself at the pet supply store — and he and I went for walks in the neighborhood, picking times when most of our neighbors would be at school or at work, or in the evenings when it would be harder for someone to see us clearly as we walked past.

I hadn't met any of my immediate neighbors yet. They kept to themselves almost as if they, too, were in the Witness Security Program. Perhaps they were. It would make sense for the U.S. Marshals Service to buy up entire neighborhoods to house people who were in hiding, so long as they didn't know each other from their previous lives.

No curious neighbors to pick apart a new resident's story. No concerns about accidental recognition when everyone is concentrating on lying low and not being seen by anyone else.

I remembered moving when really young, which it seems we did fairly often. Every time we settled into a new neighborhood, the folks from next door or across the street, or around the corner, would show up at the front door with a pie or cookies or something else, welcoming the newcomers to their community. If nothing else, they'd ask us what church we attended and invite us to theirs.

Once upon a time, there was even something called the Welcome Wagon, a business that employed "hostesses" to visit newcomers to a community, presenting them with a gift basket containing free samples, coupons and promotional materials from participating local businesses. I understand this ended in the late 1990s — in the United States, anyway — when it became harder to catch newcomers at home and interest dropped off.

Times have changed and people don't visit new neighbors as much anymore. The last time I'd moved, before everything in my life went to hell, there were no pies or cookies, although I did get asked a time or two about my religious affiliation.

But there used to be invitations to neighborhood parties or other get-togethers. Invitations to bridge clubs, or bowling nights, or for a round of golf at the municipal golf course — all things of the past now, I guess — I remember some rollicking backyard barbecues when I was young, but not anymore.

Neighbors don't know each other now. Not unless there has been a crime spree and, out of self-interest, neighborhood watch groups are formed.

Everyone gets together and listens to a police officer make suggestions about keeping an eye on each other's property, and calling in the authorities if they ever notice anything unusual taking place.

The neighbors go home and set up signs saying they are in a neighborhood watch group, and then they go back to business as usual now that the moment of security theater has been observed. It's nice to feel safe without actually having to do anything.

In this neighborhood, because of the creature I saw in my crawlspace, I decided to pay attention, the old-fashioned way of doing things.

As Fred and I strolled around, for the air, or for exercise, or so he could sniff the trees and fire hydrants to get the latest canine news and leave a dripping message of his own, I made note of cars parked in driveways versus those parked in the street, of lawns that were neatly trimmed versus those overgrown with weeds, of basketball goals and badminton nets and hopscotch grids drawn in chalk on sidewalks and trash containers left at the side of the street instead of being returned to the side of the house after they were emptied.

A few curtains moved in windows as we walked by. A few people walking to their cars said hi to us after I had greeted them first.

At one point, a couple of children playing in a yard came over to greet Fred.

"Does he bite?" the older one, a girl, asked. She wore a yellow dress and had a matching yellow ribbon in her blond hair.

I stepped back, stroking my stubbled chin, trying to put a thoughtful look on my face. "Depends," I said.

"Depends on what?" She asked. A younger boy, I assumed her brother, stepped closer. He wore a blue-and-white striped T-shirt and dark blue shorts, and was as blond as the girl.

"Depends on whether you two are lizard people disguised as children," I said.

Now Fred took a step back, looking at me, then at the two children.

"What is 'dis' ... 'dis' thingy mean?" The boy asked.

The girl turned to him and said, "It means are we wearing children costumes like at Halloween when we are really lizards inside."

The boy turned all serious and said to Fred and me, "I'm a real boy, see?" He raised his T-shirt, exposing a rounded belly with an outie belly button. Fred stepped forward and gave it a good, wet lick.

The boy squeaked in surprise and jumped back, but his sister laughed and reached forward to pet Fred.

Fred let her. And when the boy stepped forward again, giggling, Fred allowed himself to be petted some more.

I felt the eyes of watchful adults on us. "C'mon, Fred, we've got a train to catch," I said. The boy and girl waved at us as Fred and I continued our walk.

Around the corner, I noticed Fred was watching me. "Wondering about the train?" I asked. He huffed a small bark, meaning yes. "It was just something to say to give us an excuse to move on."

He continued to stare at me. "OK, Fred, it was a lie," I admitted. He stopped and looked back the way we'd come. Then I realized he wasn't mad at me about my lying. Or at least that wasn't the entire reason he was upset.

"You were enjoying the attention, weren't you?" I asked. He looked up at me, then lay down where he stood.

I knelt and loved on him, stroking his back, scratching behind his ears, massaging his shoulders. "I'm sorry, Fred. I was being thoughtless."

He jumped to his feet, barked, and resumed walking as if nothing had happened. I guess I was forgiven. Now it was time for us to move on.

And so we did.

All-in-all, the neighbors pretty much kept to themselves and Fred and I did nothing intentionally to draw them out.

At least, not yet.

CHAPTER 7: THE THING

The sun's last rays tinted the partly cloudy sky in bright colors as Fred and I went out for a stroll, and I marveled at the reds, oranges and yellows as the blue gave way to purple and then star-studded darkness. I felt a moment of sympathy for Fred because as a dog he didn't have the same color sense, and he couldn't enjoy the sunset the way I did.

What I didn't think of at first was that his other senses — which are far superior to my own — had kicked into high gear once he caught a sniff of something on the breeze.

"'Is way," he said, tugging on the leash to go left. Usually we turned right upon leaving the house.

"Something?" I asked softly.

"Yeh!" he huffed, and we proceeded to go on our walk, him leading me instead of me guiding him by the leash.

In this neighborhood, the blocks are much longer than the ones I remembered exploring as a child. Instead of maybe six houses between cross streets on a block, we'd pass by a dozen before reaching the next street. I guess that's big city neighborhoods versus small town blocks. The streetlights also were set far apart, at night leaving vast pools of darkness in the center of each block, broken only by porch lights or soft interior light that managed to escape despite curtained windows.

The houses were all variations on the same theme, built during the same post-World War II building boom as mine. Some were two stories, with bedrooms added above the built-in garage, and others were just a single story. Through the years many occupants had tired of painting the wood siding of their houses every few years or after a punishing hail storm, and had opted for either aluminum or vinyl siding. Although I did see one house that still appeared to be covered with ugly green asbestos shingles — it surprised me that those still existed in this anti-asbestos age. Its roof was covered by the same asphalt composition shingles as its neighbors, so if a raging fire were to sweep through the neighborhood, those asbestos shingles would be no good against the flames.

Fred stopped at the eighth house down, which appeared in the gathering evening to be covered with a light tan vinyl siding, and he sniffed around a tree in the front yard. After marking the tree with a message for the next dog to come along, he advanced no farther on our walk, instead staring at the house.

I knelt beside him and stroked his back. He was vibrating like a violin string about to snap.

"Is it here?"

"Yeh!"

"Under?"

"Nuh!"

"Inside?"

"Yeh!"

I glanced around at the neighboring houses. All was quiet.

Most folks were probably preparing or eating dinner, or gathered around their TVs for whatever game show or reality show or police procedural was grabbing their attention. Not a twitch from the curtains in any window. No shadowy person grabbing an after-dinner smoke on their front porch.

This house looked pretty much the same as the rest. An SUV was in the driveway, but several rolled newspapers had collected around its rear tires. The trash container was still at the edge of the street, although collection day was two days ago. Despite the gloom I could see envelopes sticking out of the mailbox beside the front door; it looked like several days' worth.

"Stay here and keep an eye out, Fred," I said.

He huffed softly and backed to the tree so he could watch the street without worrying about something or someone sneaking up from behind.

Smart dog!

I practiced blending with shadows as I moved up to the SUV and in front to the garage door. I worked the latch and found it unlocked. Fortunately, it wasn't an automatic door. I pulled it up slowly, as quietly as I could, until a gap was opened large enough for me to slip inside. Then I eased the door down again from the inside.

Several days earlier, I'd purchased a new flashlight that was advertised as a "High Performance Flashlight!" Yes, complete with the exclamation mark. It promised to be 40 times brighter than a regular flashlight, and came in five modes: high beam, medium beam and low beam, plus strobe and, as an added feature, a flashing S-O-S.

And it ran on just three AAA batteries. By pulling the head of the flashlight forward, I could zoom the light to an even tighter beam.

It's advertised to be bright enough that the light could be seen from five nautical miles away; you may have seen the commercials on late-night TV. It also warns against shining the light directly into your eyes. In the Lumens measurement of light output, it was rated at 600 in its brightest mode.

I know this sounds like an advertisement for the flashlight, but I assure you it is totally uncompensated. You just need to know what it can do so you'll understand better what was about to happen.

I figured it had to be better than the cheap penlight I'd used in the crawlspace under my house.

I switched it on to the lowest setting and masked even that glow with my gloved hand to keep the illumination at a minimum. I saw why the garage wasn't used to park the SUV. It was full of boxes stacked shoulder high.

A hoarder, perhaps, or someone stocking merchandise they hoped to sell on eBay or some other online sales site, I figured.

I threaded my way through the maze to the back of the garage, where I expected to find a door into the house. And there it was, also unlocked, next to a washer and dryer.

People may be certain to lock their front doors and back doors nowadays, but not so much the other doors like these. Too inconvenient, I suppose.

Flashlight off, I eased the door open slowly and peeped into the kitchen. No light was on, but a glow filtered in through the windows from outside. Night had fallen completely by now, but the neighbors on the other side of the yard had their back patio light on, which gave me enough illumination to see the kitchen was empty.

I stepped around a breakfast table and chairs and looked through the next open doorway, which led into the living room and entryway. I tried to emulate Fred, listening for any tiniest sound as my human eyes made out only shadows of furniture in the dark room. Not a peep, nor a rustle, nor even an exhalation from someone in a deep sleep. It was still early, really. Rare for everyone in a house to be asleep at this time. Maybe they were on vacation somewhere.

I breathed through my mouth to improve my hearing — breathing through one's nose brings the movement of air too close to the ears and can affect how well one hears.

No mindless chatter from a television, nor from a radio talk show. No video game chaos. No idle chatter between siblings or low murmurs between lovers trying not to disturb the children.

I sniffed the air, carefully, quietly. The odor of decomposition was strong, coming from down a hallway leading away from the kitchen toward what I figured were the bedrooms.

I felt my way through the darkness. The light from the neighbor's back patio only reached so far, and here in the hallway it was almost pitch black. I placed my feet carefully, not wanting to step on or trip over a child's toy or basket of clothing or anything else that might have been left in the hallway when it was still bright enough to see.

No flashlight, because I didn't want to give warning to anyone — or anything — that I was in the house with them. If all was well, I wanted to be able to retreat without anyone knowing I'd visited.

If all wasn't well ...

Well, it wasn't.

I came to a bedroom. The door was open and some light from outside — a street light, or the glow of a neighbor's porch light, perhaps — filtered in through the curtains. I could see the shape of a bed, and the shape of someone on the bed, and the shape of someone or something leaning over the side of the bed.

To hell with it, I decided. I aimed the flashlight as if it were a pistol and switched on the beam.

The next few moments were crazy fast.

My main impressions were that the figure leaning over the bed jerked upright and shrieked, and I was stunned by the loudness of its shriek. So stunned, in fact, that I dropped the flashlight. The figure rushed at me still shrieking and slammed into me like a cannonball. I was knocked to the floor and the shadowy figure went through the doorway. My flashlight, still on, came to rest shining on my face, blinding me until I could scramble for it and turn the bright beam away. The person on the bed didn't move, not even when I decided to go for broke and switched on the overhead light.

It was a child, pale as death. Boy or girl, I couldn't immediately say, not really wanting to look any closer beyond the throat that had been ripped open. Savagely, brutally ripped open, not with the nicety of a scalpel stroke, but by fangs wielded with a furious intent.

Then I realized, I'd seen this child just recently. It was the girl who, with her younger brother, had proved they weren't lizard people so they could pet Fred.

Sick at heart, I turned back to the hallway, to the sea of darkness that lay beyond the bright island of light that was the dead girl's bedroom.

I heard Fred bark once outside. The neighbors probably had heard the shrieking and were responding.

I shut off the bedroom light.

There's a feeling you get at times like this. You make a mistake and recognize it instantly for what it is, then your heart drops into your stomach as you realize you can't undo the mistake, because trying to do so would be an even bigger mistake. It freezes you in place, cements your feet to the floor as the fight or flight hormones feed into your blood supply and you realize you can neither fight nor take flight.

I was in a darkened room with a dead body, or bodies — I wondered about the girl's brother, and the parents who had watched to make certain I wasn't going to be molesting their children — in a darkened house occupied by a predator. The house had to stay dark if I was to remain undiscovered by neighbors alerted by the shrieks, yet keeping it dark was to the advantage of the predator that even now could be stalking me.

And how was I going to get out without being seen by the neighbors? Even if a neighborhood watch program were not currently active in this area, long-time neighbors do know each other and will respond to sounds of distress. Like a shrill shriek in the night.

I knew Fred was smart enough to stay out of sight, so at least I didn't need to worry about him.

It was my throat, on one hand, and my freedom, on the other, that were of concern to me.

Think! *Think!*

I crouched down, making myself as small a target as possible, and stuck my head through the doorway into the hall. The hallway was as dark as before, but

I could see a lessening of the darkness coming from the kitchen area, where the neighbor's patio light still shone.

In the other direction, total darkness.

I sniffed the air. The smell of rot was strong, but not overwhelming.

So the creature wasn't lying in wait, practically on top of me, then.

I stayed low and scurried down the hallway to the kitchen, then stopped and whirled to look back, halfway expecting the creature to be there, about to pounce. Too many scary movies, I guess.

The creature did not appear to be stalking me from the darkness — but even if it was, I just couldn't see it.

I retraced my steps past the breakfast table in the kitchen to the doorway to the garage.

Inside the maze of boxes, the smell of rot was stronger. Had the creature taken refuge here? Was it lying in wait for me?

I didn't want to be trapped by either the creature or the neighbors, who I could hear from outside as they approached the front door, calling out to, I assumed, the people who lived here.

The kitchen had another door on the other side, leading out to the back yard. But it was well illuminated by the neighbor's patio light, and I would be seen leaving that way.

I couldn't use a window; people tend to notice when somebody climbs out of a window after they've been alerted by someone shrieking.

The garage was it then.

I could hear the neighbors gathering outside. They were at the front door, knocking and calling out, ringing the doorbell.

I had one chance.

Ignoring the predator, hoping it would do me the same courtesy, I quickly threaded the maze of boxes to the main garage door, using my flashlight's low setting to light the way. At the door, I switched it off.

I took a deep breath. This'd better work!

I knew the garage door was in the dark, partially hidden from sight by the SUV parked in front of it. If no one was standing by the door, or looking in this direction ...

I jerked and lifted the garage door and stepped through onto the driveway as if I were opening it from the outside, and yelled, "Here's a way in!"

Fred barked from beside me, with the end of the leash in his mouth, and I accepted it from him just as a neighbor's flashlight caught me in its beam. I hoped I looked just like someone who had been walking his dog, who had responded with the others to the sound of a shriek.

"Over here," I heard someone say, and the crowd at the front door moved my direction.

"That's pretty clever," someone said.

I nodded. "Yeah, I was walking my dog when I heard that, whatever it was, and figured the garage door might be a way in if the front door was locked."

They accepted me, and several neighbors who knew the family advanced into the garage.

I caught a glimpse of a small, dark figure as it slipped out of the garage and disappeared into the darkness around the corner, and I knew the predator was free to stalk and kill again.

Fred and I also faded into the background and resumed our walk down the street as the neighbors continued to collect outside the house. We were on the next block when the emergency sirens became audible, and by the time we returned home from a neighboring street, the eighth house down was lighted up like a midnight crime scene.

Before turning toward the house, Fred stopped at the sidewalk, watching the activity down the street. I crouched beside him, stroking down his back.

"Thinking of the children who met you the other day?" I asked, quietly.

Fred huffed a soft bark.

"That was their house," I said.

He looked into my eyes, whined, then turned toward our house. "Yeah, Fred. Me too," I said. "Me too."

CHAPTER 8: CALLING IN

I had U.S. Marshal Penny Ransome's personal telephone number memorized. She didn't want me calling it, but I called anyway.

"What is it, Carter? The raccoon come back?"

"You might say that," I said.

Fred was getting a drink of water. I put the phone on speaker as soon as he was done.

I had an ounce of scotch at hand, but had done nothing but pour it so far.

"It might be too late for the morning papers, but the local TV news is probably going to lead with what happened just down the street from me," I said.

"I told you not to draw attention," she said.

"I didn't. At least, I'm trying not to. This just happened."

She sighed. She does that a lot when dealing with me. "OK, what's going on?"

"Fred and I were on our regular evening walk — we are allowed to do that, aren't we?"

"We'll see."

"Well, Fred stopped and told me he smelled the same thing that was under the house the other day; only it was at a place eight houses down from me."

"Go on."

"I ... ah ... I found a way into the house ..."

"Uh-huh."

"And, to make a long story short, I found a body."

"A body."

"Yes. A girl Fred and I met the other day. Her throat was ripped out."

"As she had been attacked by a rabid raccoon?"

"You might say that, except — Penny, I saw it, and it was no raccoon."

"Not a raccoon."

"No, not a raccoon."

"Carter, I thought you were going to keep this long story short."

"Sorry! I ... ah ... you know, I'd rather you were here, looking me in the face as I told you this."

"Well, I'm not. Spill it!"

"Yes, Ma'am. You know those old movies. Not just the old black-and-white movies, but the silent ones?"

"Carter ..."

"I'm getting to it. I just need to be sure it's put in context. Look. There was an old, old, silent movie made in the early 1920s in Germany, titled *Nosferatu*."

"Nose ... what?"

"*Nosferatu*. It was a somewhat derivative version of Bram Stoker's *Dracula* by someone who didn't have the rights to use the actual story. The vampire in the film didn't look like Bela Lugosi's Dracula. 'Count Orlok,' portrayed by Max Schreck, was a hideous creature with close-set fangs in front, and long, claw-like fingers. Pale white and — I did say hideous, didn't I?"

"Wait a minute! You're saying this is a vampire?" She sounded incredulous. I didn't blame her.

"An actual vampire? I don't know. I don't think so. I guess. It was bent over the girl, and the girl's throat was ripped out. But was it drinking the blood? I can't say for certain."

"Vampires don't exist."

I looked at Fred and spoke without thinking. "Neither do talking dogs."

Penny said nothing. I had her there.

Fred just huffed.

"Look, here are the facts as I've observed them. This thing, this creature, whatever it is, smells like rotting flesh. It got into this house and apparently ripped out the throat of this girl. I figure there are more dead people inside the house; I didn't stick around to find out. Low profile and all. Oh, and apparently it doesn't like bright light; I caught it in the dark and gave it a bright beam from my flashlight and it shrieked and fled the room."

"How bright is your flashlight?"

"It's supposed to be 600 Lumens, and is advertised to be visible from five nautical miles away. It could probably blind something that prefers the darkness." I didn't tell her how it blinded me as well.

"I'll reserve judgment for now on whatever this thing is. You think more than one death is involved?"

"The house has at least three bedrooms. This was the girl alone in one of the bedrooms. I'm guessing two adults and at least one maybe two more children?"

"Ah, crap!" she said.

"Yeah," I said.

"Well, as U.S. Marshals, we don't have jurisdiction for something like this, so I can't go barging in on the investigation." She paused in thought for a moment, then continued. "But I can put out some feelers and see what sort of information I can get. Meanwhile ... you stay put! If you must take Fred for a walk, take him to a park or something and try to avoid contact with other people in your neighborhood. Let the local authorities take care of this ... whatever it is."

"I hear you," I said.

"'I hear you,'" she repeated. "Which means you aren't going to do what I tell you."

"Penny, I can't give you a blanket promise. This thing was *under my house*. It could have been me lying here with my throat ripped out. And that was a child Fred and I met. If some way comes up that I can act on this, without drawing attention to myself, I'll do it. Otherwise, I'm out of it, OK?"

"If you get yourself killed — and that's what will happen if you call attention to yourself — then everything you've done back here will be for naught. Stay out of the light, stay healthy, and stay safe."

"Yes, Mother."

"Cut that out!"

CHAPTER 9: THE COVER-UP

Fred and I were still awake at 6 a.m. when the early local news came on the TV. As I'd predicted, the deaths down the street led the broadcast.

But not as I'd expected.

"A family of five has died in their sleep as a result of carbon monoxide poisoning, police say," the chipper blonde told her sleepy audience, as video showed sheet-draped bodies being removed from the house down the street. Lights strobing red and blue and white reflected in a semi-random sequence off the front of the house in the darkness, so you couldn't quite tell what color it was.

A fire department spokesman told a TV reporter about the importance of functioning carbon monoxide alarms, and a couple of neighbors discussed how tragic it was that such a thing could happen to people they knew. Then a sober medical doctor, standing in front of a sign pointing to an emergency room, described symptoms of carbon monoxide poisoning and what you should do if you suspect you are being poisoned by the noxious fumes in your own home.

I switched the TV off. There was no need to check the newscasts on other channels. The fix was in. The authorities were covering up the cause of death, probably to avoid starting a panic. Whether the media were in on it or not was immaterial.

I could understand that; was familiar with it, in fact.

Once upon a time, I might have been terrified had I learned that a neighbor had died after having her throat ripped out. As it turns out though, my neighbor — who was also my lover — was executed with two bullets to the head and buried in a nearby wooded area.

But that was in the past, where I hoped to keep it, and a thousand miles away, maybe more. Ancient history, from the days before I was "Earl Carter" and Fred was "Fred."

Cover-up or not, I was privy to certain information that the average city resident was not. But what could I do?

I thought about the face I'd seen. Oval, pale, with big eyes, and what looked like fangs set close together protruding from its mouth. A resemblance to Count Orlock, yet after further reflection not all that similar. Almost otherworldly, or just not entirely human. A vampire? Really?

Everything I knew about vampires — if that's really what this thing was — I learned from fiction. From the pages of 19th-century works by Bram Stoker as well as more modern depictions by Anne Rice, Chelsea Quinn Yarbro and Charlaine Harris, I had a lot of likely useless information about the undead.

And I didn't even know if this creature was a vampire of legend, or just some unfortunate soul with hygiene problems who was driven into a murderous rage after being infected by rabies.

If even that.

It wasn't all that big, come to think of it, although it had been big enough for its momentum to knock me over. A dwarf vampire? How absurd! And yet ...

Fred and I checked every access point into the house, with special attention to the fireplace, before finally going to bed.

We did not sleep well at all that night, or rather, early morning.

CHAPTER 10: CALL BACK

Penny's call awakened me around 1 p.m. I put it on speaker so Fred could hear.

"I'm told the family — the Andersons, two parents, a 6-month-old daughter, 4-year-old son and 9-year-old daughter — all died of carbon monoxide poisoning," she said.

"Yeah," I said, laying on the sarcasm. "I've never heard of carbon monoxide poisoning causing throats to burst open."

"Of course not," she said. "To determine the victims died of carbon monoxide poisoning so quickly, they would have had to run blood tests immediately to determine the amount of CO in their systems. But it's hard to run a blood test when there is no blood to test."

"None?"

"None," she said.

"They were drained?"

"It looks that way. Investigators are thinking they were killed elsewhere, their bodies drained of blood, then they were brought home and placed in their beds as if they'd been sleeping when they were attacked."

"Some sort of bizarre terrorist act?"

"Possibly," she said. "They're hoping by claiming CO poisoning, they'll drive the guilty parties to speak up and claim the attack."

"That's a good one," I said.

"They're looking at the first people into the house as possibly being involved in it."

"That's absurd!"

"It's a way of preventing them from blurting to their friends and neighbors that it wasn't CO poisoning, but something much, much worse that killed this family."

"So ... when they are released from questioning, they'll parrot the poisoning story to avoid further suspicion."

"Exactly."

"People in law enforcement are devious," I said.

"From you, Carter, I'll take that as a compliment."

"So what about the real killer?"

She paused before speaking, clearly reluctant to say it aloud: "A 'vampire'? They'd have to catch it in the act to prove it, and even then they wouldn't believe what they see. They'll write it off as someone high on bath salts or some new designer drug."

"So do you believe in vampires now?" I asked, not even sure that I did myself. It was all so bizarre.

She said, "I believe in talking dogs."

Fred huffed.

CHAPTER 11: A WALK IN THE PARK

Fred and I considered going for a walk down the block again that evening, but reconsidered when we saw how busy the neighborhood had become. People were out in their yards, talking to each other, or sitting on their porches, watching. Just watching. The official word might have been carbon monoxide poisoning, but the people on this block were not taking the officials at their word.

So Fred and I bundled into my car and we drove to a nearby park, as Penny had suggested.

It was not busy. Years ago apparently, the city had imposed a curfew on parks between 11 p.m. and 6 a.m., citing vandalism, drug use and other crimes as reasons for keeping people out of the public parks overnight. Fred and I arrived at 8:30 p.m. to find the park all but deserted.

I wondered if maybe word of the violent deaths had spread enough to dissuade people from venturing far from their homes after dark. Although the deaths *did* occur at home, not in a park. Man, the rational animal, really isn't as rational as he likes to think.

This park had a sidewalk that meandered through trees and around shrubs, in and out of the yellow light of old-fashioned lampposts set up around the perimeter, with a lighted playground area in the center. Fred and I walked silently along for the most part, stopping now and then for him to read and leave messages on the canine news network.

I half expected him to stop as he had the night before and announce that he'd detected the creature. It might happen in a TV show, perhaps, but not this time. Our stroll through the park was uneventful and we returned home without incident.

But I spent a large part of the time thinking about the creature and how it apparently hunted.

Say, for the sake of argument, that it *was* a vampire — if such a thing could actually exist. Throw out all we supposedly know from literature and folklore, and concentrate on the evidence before us.

No romantic sparkling, no coffin filled with soil from back home, no fear of crossing rushing waters, no aversion to garlic, no great sexual attraction with the living, no ability to fly or to shift into the form of other creatures, no requirement that one has to be invited into your home before it can enter. All the rules of fiction, broken and discarded.

This thing stank like rotting meat. It appeared to prefer the darkness and exhibited extreme discomfort upon being caught in the bright beam of a tactical flashlight. It ripped throats out and apparently drained bodies of their blood, instead of daintily nipping the flesh and sucking a pint or two at a time. It was capable of moving quietly and of choosing its victims — perhaps preferring those who sleep over those who were awake and could fight back.

Was it sentient? Or was it acting on some predatory instinct? Could it pass its condition on to others? Or was it some predator that had successfully avoided detection, classification, and eradication through centuries of coexistence with humanity? Was it a blood-sucking alien from outer space or some alternate dimension? Or a mutated mosquito that was too big to fly to its next meal?

Too many questions, not enough answers.

I didn't even know why it was under my house when Fred first detected it. If I hadn't had Fred, my impossible talking dog, I never would have known about this creature under my floor.

When we got home, I told Fred, "In the morning, we're going to go back under the house and see what we can figure out about this thing."

He didn't say anything, just looked at me and wagged his tail. He'd already figured out what we needed to do. I told you he was smart.

He accompanied me as I made my rounds, confirming all doors and windows were sealed, all closets and other hiding places were empty, and the bed was safe for sleeping. He curled up in my armpit and rested his chin on my shoulder, and we fell asleep that way.

CHAPTER 12: BACK UNDER

Come morning, after a hearty breakfast and, despite the hour and a touch of misgiving, a wee bit o' scotch to boost my courage — Fred was just fine without it — he and I returned to the crawlspace under the house.

I brought the tactical flashlight this time instead of the penlight I'd used earlier. I wanted to see what I was dealing with — if there was anything down there — and having a flashlight known to make the creature shriek and flee made me feel a bit more comfortable about going back under the house.

"OK, Fred, if it has a nest under the house, let's find it," I said. I also brought along a camera, a plastic trash bag and a small shovel made for backpacking.

Fred huffed and this time led the way under the house. A good sign the creature hadn't returned, I thought, as I followed and lighted his path.

We crawled the distance under the house to the base of the chimney, and Fred indicated this was the place to look. He also sneezed, glanced at me, then made a hasty retreat to several feet away.

I could tell why as I got closer. It reeked of creature, of the rot and decay of something that should have been buried in a deep grave, or covered with lime to eat the stink away. I figured this must be what zombies would smell like, if they existed.

Beside the base of the chimney, in the soft soil, was a sort of nest, a shallow depression capable of holding a creature the size of a miniature poodle or a toddler. It was lined with tattered and stinking pieces of cloth, too filthy to allow a determination as to their source.

I brought up the camera and used it to photograph the nest from several different angles. I then employed the shovel and trash bag, and I packaged the nesting materials securely inside the plastic.

Then Fred and I crawled out from under the house and replaced the metal cover over the hole in the foundation.

I washed the dirt off his paws again and brushed the cobwebs out of his coat, then showered and changed into a clean set of clothing. It took a long time in the shower, under lots of soap and water, to wash the stench of the nest away.

I then called our favorite U.S. Marshal.

"Fred and I found its nest," I said. "Well, a nest, anyway. I don't think it's been back since we first discovered it under the house."

I described the nest to her and promised to email the photos and package up the stuff in the trash bag for her to have tested. This was the first physical evidence of this creature that we had — other than the ripped throats down the street — and maybe this would help with the investigation.

Assuming, that is, that the federal agency chose to communicate its findings with the local authorities. They had to treat it this way because of me. I had to stay out of the picture if I was going to remain in the picture, you might say. If the local authorities had known I had this creature's nest under my house, I would have been brought in for questioning, fingerprinted and found out.

Then I'd be dead.

Fred and I left some pretty bad enemies behind us. Worse, even, than this throat-ripping bloodsucker. Hard to imagine, huh?

I double-bagged, then triple-bagged the nest, and still the smell seemed to seep through the packaging material. Apparently the plastic in trash bags wasn't as impermeable to gases as I thought. Whew, what a stench!

I put the package inside a fourth bag lined with fresh-ground coffee mixed with baking soda, then gave up on trying to mask the odor any further.

After shipping the package off, I called Penny again and explained the reasons for the extra packaging plus the coffee grounds and baking soda. "I swear to you the white powder is not anthrax," I said.

She used my word, "Gotcha," which told me this amused her.

"OK, now I've got a question for you. What do you know about this house, before I moved in? Why would it harbor a nest for this thing, without the previous occupants noticing that disgusting odor coming from under the floor?"

"I can't answer that."

"Can't? Or won't?"

"Can't. I'll have to do a little research and get back to you on that," she said. "All I know at present is that this house was acquired in an asset confiscation and remodeled and turned into a safe house for use by the Witness Security Program. You are the first person in the program to occupy that particular house."

"Lucky me," I said.

"And lucky me, since I get to deal with you on this. Remember what I told you ..."

"Yep! Stay out of trouble, stay healthy and don't go near the light, or something like that."

CHAPTER 13: ABOUT FRED

My beard continued to grow, as beards have a tendency to do, and I kept the dye job touched up as needed.

It's harder to disguise a dog than it is a man, so Fred's appearance was pretty much unchanged. I'd refused to let them dock his tail or cut and break his ears to reset them standing upright, like a Doberman's. Fred was wearing a different-color collar — that leather one he'd selected at the pet supply store — and that would have to be enough to change his looks.

They'd tried to split us up, warning me that Fred's presence greatly increased the risk of discovery, but I'd argued that the risk was worth it because I was never going to let Fred go.

And Fred had made it pretty clear to Penny, too, that he felt the same way.

There's nothing like a miracle to get someone to advocate on your behalf.

And Fred's being able to talk was indeed a miracle. I'm not talking about divine intervention or anything like that. Fred's being able to talk was pretty much a miracle of breeding and selection, with perhaps a stray burst of cosmic radiation acting on his chromosomes when he was still a satisfied gleam in his sire's eye.

The breeder I'd gotten him from had been working with dogs that showed a propensity for vocalizing, and mixed them with dogs known for their intelligence and ability to solve problems.

Fred was the runt of the litter and, as such, had to work harder than all his brothers and sisters to get his mother's attention and access to a nipple.

When weaned from his mother and adopted into a human family, he'd continued to struggle to communicate with his new pack mate. Me, in particular.

I'd chosen him out of the litter precisely because he was smart and vocal, not to mention cute as a button, and I'd worked with him to develop a vocabulary he could use and I could understand. Something much more involved than the "Ai ruvv oo" I'd heard "spoken" in YouTube videos.

And Fred (not his original name) had surprised the daylights out of me by picking up a vocabulary beyond what I'd worked up to teach him. And he had an understanding of life surrounding him that astonished me even further.

I've never told anyone this before, but he's the one who brought my conscience into play concerning the murders, drug deals and racketeering that I then was able to expose, thus resulting in our disappearing into this new life multiple states away from former friends and dysfunctional family.

Fred and his ability to talk saved my life, even as he destroyed my old life, career, friendships and family relationships. I owed everything to Fred, and there is no way I would allow anything to tear us apart.

I loved that guy, and the knowledge that, as a dog, his days were numbered terrified me no end.

We'd talk about it, late at night, usually after I'd had one too many servings of scotch. The drunker I was, the better his vocabulary and ability to pronounce words became. I don't know whether my speech perception loosened up enough to tell what he was saying, or perhaps he felt freer to express himself clearly when he knew that I wasn't thinking all that clearly myself.

"You'll be fine when I'm gone," I remember him saying one night when I was in my cups, after we'd found the dead family down the street. "You are coming along admirably in your training."

"'My training'? To do what?"

"Why, to take care of yourself, of course. You were in pretty bad shape when I came along."

"I don't understand."

"Take, for instance, your escape from the house where the bad thing was."

"I thought I was done for," I said. "I was trapped. There was no way I could escape. They'd catch me in there with that dead family, and I'd be on death row as a result."

"Before I came along, that no doubt would have been the result," Fred said. "But under my guidance, you have learned to think for yourself, to plan your actions ahead of time, and to prepare to change plans when conditions require."

"I used the expectations of the neighbors to my benefit," I recalled. "They didn't expect someone to come out of the garage and announce that he'd found a way in. They were more ready to expect someone to try the garage door from the outside, and then make the announcement."

"Exactly," Fred said. "And that is why I believe you will do just fine when I am gone. I have confidence in you."

Apparently I fell asleep at this point because I remember no further conversation.

If there really was a conversation.

If it wasn't all a dream to begin with.

CHAPTER 14: THE NEST

Penny texted me several days after I'd sent the package, saying only, "Whew! Stinks!" It had arrived.

The newspaper and television stations said no more about the carbon monoxide poisonings and, contrary to law enforcement expectations, no terrorist group announced that it had committed the murders.

Fred and I tried to get into a routine that did not match what we had done in our old life. We did a lot of walking together and frequented a sidewalk café downtown that allowed pets, and we ate foods we never would have eaten previously. Healthier foods.

I lost a lot of weight I didn't need, and Fred also seemed to become more streamlined.

Then Penny called.

"That package you sent," she said.

"Yes?"

"All it lacked were egg shells and orange rinds."

"Come again?"

"It was just garbage, Carter. Old, blood-soaked meat packages, dirty clothing, candy wrappers, the type of stuff every household produces by the ton every year. The only thing unusual about it all was what you added — the dry, unused coffee grounds and baking soda."

"You saw the photos."

"Sure. It looked like a nest, but if it was, it was a nest lined with common household garbage. The stink came from the bloody meat packages, rotting with everything else in there."

"Did the techs test the blood?"

"The hamburger packages contained beef blood; the chicken packages contained chicken blood; the pork packages ... you get the picture."

"No blood on the clothing?"

"None."

"So ... draw any conclusions?"

"Nothing I care to share at the moment," she said.

"Gotcha," I said.

Fred huffed, ran out of the room and returned a moment later with his favorite stuffed toy, a teddy bear. He'd had a tendency to tear up other stuffed toys, usually to get at the squeaker inside, but he had not harmed this one. Instead, he liked to lie down with it when taking a nap, when I wasn't also lying down.

"Umm, here's a thought, Penny. Perhaps the odors from the meat packages provided a level of comfort to this creature," I said.

"'Comfort'?"

"Sure. Fred just brought me his teddy bear, which he treats differently from other stuffed toys. It's a comfort to him, right Fred?"

"Yeh!"

"Suppose this creature lines its nest with familiar smells — rotting blood — so it feels at home when it's there. Like that TV character — what's his name? — who kept his late wife's pillow in a plastic bag so he could smell her scent from time to time."

"I remember that show. 'Monk,' with Tony Shalhoub. I loved that show. He had a cleanliness thing, obsessive-compulsive," she said.

"That's the one. Anyway, this creature clearly doesn't have a cleanliness thing, but I'd hazard a guess that it still likes to smell rotting blood."

"Which might tie in with its compulsion to drain the blood from its victims," she said.

"Is it a compulsion? It might just be the way this thing hunts and consumes its prey. Like a mosquito. Or a tick."

"Mosquitoes and ticks don't build nests."

"True, true," I admitted. "Look, we don't know enough about this thing to be able to say whether it's operating on instinct or some higher level of thought and reason. Although ..."

She waited for me to continue my thought, and when I didn't continue, she asked, a little impatiently I felt, "'Although' what?"

"Maybe we do know a little more about this creature than I realized."

"Such as?"

"I don't remember telling you about leaving the house after I discovered the body."

"You just said you ... um ... 'didn't stick around.'"

"OK, here's the deal. I found the creature bending over a bed with its victim, the girl."

"I'm guessing the 9-year-old. Go on."

"The 9-year-old, right. I flicked on the high beam of my flashlight, and it shrieked as if in pain. It rushed at me — I don't think it was attacking me. I think it was just trying to get out of the room and away from the light, and I was blocking the only exit."

"No, you didn't tell me any of this, Carter."

"It knocked me down. I dropped the flashlight, and it ended up shining on me, blinding me."

"And at the same time protecting you from this creature," she said. "Maybe it didn't want to get into the light even if it wanted to eliminate you as a threat."

"Hmm, good point. Anyway, Fred barked from out front and I knew the neighbors had to be responding to the shrieks. I turned off the flashlight ..."

"Giving up your only defense against that thing."

"Yeah, I thought of that. But I didn't want the neighbors seeing a moving light inside the house, and come bursting in to find me and five dead bodies."

"How do you know there were five bodies?"

"I didn't at the time. I heard it on the news, afterward, and you mentioned it as well."

"Gotcha," she said.

"I had come in through the garage — when they aren't automatic, those doors are so seldom locked — and figured that was the only way I could get out. Even then, it would be a gamble. When I got to the garage, I could smell the creature."

"It was in the garage," Penny said, beating me to the punch line.

"It was in the garage," I said anyway.

"Penny, it didn't attack me," I continued. "It hid and let me do my thing, and after I opened the door, it escaped into the darkness."

"You were awake, on your feet, and carrying a weapon it knew could hurt it."

"That's what I was thinking. It strikes me as being more than just acting on instinct."

"Not necessarily," she said. "It might just prefer its prey to be sleeping and helpless. That doesn't take intellect, if millions of years of evolution led it to feeding on the unwary."

I paused to take this in and think about it, then said, "Are you arguing now that it's an animal operating solely on instinct? What happened to the compulsion you were talking about?"

"I think I can see both sides of the issue. Just like you, Carter. I'm just going to have to reserve judgment until we know more about this thing."

I heard a buzzing sound in Penny's background, and she continued, "Look, Carter, I've got to go. Talk to you soon."

I hung up and looked at Fred. "What do you think, buddy?"

He grinned at me and panted, wagging his tail.

"You and me both, Fred. You and me both."

He picked up his teddy bear and trotted out of the room with it. When he didn't come back, I figured it was nap time, so I got up to do some kitchen chores. I had second thoughts along the way and checked on him in the bedroom.

Fred was on the bed all right, curled around the teddy bear, but with his head lying on the pillow where I usually lay my head at night. He raised his head and looked at me.

"Have a nice nap, Fred," I said, and returned to my chores, neglected no longer.

CHAPTER 15: SPECULATION

That night, I dreamed of River, the neighbor from my former life, the one who was killed with two bullets in the head. Except this time, Bela Lugosi was ripping his fangs into her throat and sucking the lifeblood out of her.

I knew it wasn't right. I'd witnessed the murder and it had played over and over in my head, day and night, for the longest time, and there was no vampire involved. Just my father, the police lieutenant who was also a local drug lord, who had decided to make a statement, punctuating it with two 9mm rounds.

He didn't drag her body out to the woods to bury it. He gave that job to me.

In my dream, she rose from the grave. In real life, I almost joined her there.

I jerked awake, shaking with a feeling that her dead, clammy fingers were still clutching my arm.

Fred was watching me. "Bad," he said.

"Bad," I agreed, and we got up together to make the rounds of the house, checking windows and doors, closets and under the bed.

Then we returned to the living room and I stood there, staring at the fireplace.

The creature had nested under it until Fred detected it and we rousted it from its hiding place. Had it been feeding?

Had there been other "carbon monoxide" deaths in the city before my neighbors down the street added to the statistics?

It consumed the blood of two adults and three children. Was it all in one night, or was it over a period of time? I remembered seeing several newspapers in the driveway and more mail in the mailbox than normal, which suggested it had been there over a period of time.

So this creature had a way of paralyzing its victims without killing them, at least until it had satiated itself and they were drained dry. Fred and I had just happened across it as it was finishing its last meal in the house.

A tick will lie in wait somewhere off the ground, in a bush, on a low tree limb, maybe on the end of a blade of grass, until a suitable source of food comes along. The tick is blind, but it can sense its prey by the presence of rising carbon dioxide levels as the warm-blooded host draws near, and it will latch on and find a good spot to settle down for a picnic, burrowing its head deep into the skin and sucking up as much blood as it can carry.

The tick, when satiated — if not discovered and removed before then — will withdraw from its host on its own and drop off. Depending on its stage in life, it may molt and go through a transformation from larva to nymph, or from nymph to adult. And if it's an adult and female, it will take the opportunity to lay thousands of eggs, launching the life cycle all over again. The adult male breeds, then dies, but the adult female may stick around a few more seasons and lay even more eggs.

This creature wasn't a tick — it could see, and was too damned big. But it had been nesting under my house before going out and dining on the blood of five victims, after which, if it had sought other victims, we hadn't heard about them yet.

So like a tick, perhaps, it was satisfied and lying low, digesting its meal.

Molting, maybe, changing from one form to another. Laying eggs, if an adult female, assuming it could have gotten them fertilized — assuming also that its species reproduced in that manner.

I didn't think there were any eggs under my house. I hoped not, anyway. Fred didn't indicate anything out of the ordinary and I was comfortable with that.

But if this creature were laying eggs somewhere else, or had already done so in the time that had passed since I'd inadvertently helped it escape from the garage, "carbon monoxide" deaths might be increasing on a grand scale in the near future.

"Fred," I said, "I think we —"

The phone rang. At 3:17 a.m.

It was Penny.

CHAPTER 16: POSSIBILITIES

"Sorry to wake you, Carter," she said.

"Already up," I said. "Fred and I couldn't sleep."

"I've found out more about the house. If you want to move out, we can make arrangements."

"What do you mean?"

"It turns out the last occupants of your house were using it to cook methamphetamines."

"A meth house," I said.

"That's right."

"That means it was filled with toxic chemicals while they were cooking. The entire interior was contaminated." I looked at the walls, freshly painted just before I'd moved in, and the wall-to-wall carpeting, still out-gassing the brand-new smell it brought from the factory. "The feds acquired the house, cleaned it up, remodeled it and turned it into a witness program safe house, right?"

"You got it."

"Let me guess something else. The previous occupants were found dead, their throats ripped out, their bodies drained of blood. But it was determined to be death by carbon monoxide poisoning."

"No, meth overdose, but you've got the rest of it right. That's why I called."

I hesitated for a moment, then asked what was on my mind: "Penny, what do you know about ticks?"

I explained to her my musings about the creature, drawing parallels from the arachnid — yes, a cousin to the spider — that survived by bleeding its victims.

"So this thing fed off the meth addicts and nested under the house while government contractors fumigated and decontaminated and redecorated the interior," I suggested, "then Fred and I moved in and accidentally evicted it."

"That makes sense," Penny admitted.

"Then, when it was hungry again, it found another house filled with vulnerable prey and, perhaps, ate its fill again. For whatever reason, it didn't go for my throat when it had a chance."

"Bright light, Carter. Don't forget the bright light."

"OK, so I still might have been prey, just not convenient at that moment. And I was useful in helping it escape from the garage at the same time I did, whether it planned it that way or it was just coincidental. In any case, I haven't heard of any more 'carbon monoxide' deaths lately, so we can probably assume it's gone to nest again somewhere else."

"Laying eggs this time?"

"God, I hope not! But what about finding a mate to fertilize them?"

"You seem to know a lot about ticks. What else do you remember from your biology classes?"

"I didn't take biology." I glanced down at Fred. He wagged his tail, but slowly. "But I have had to deal with ticks."

"OK, then, let me tell you something I picked up in biology. There are some species that don't have to rely on an opposite sex to fertilize their eggs. They reproduce through parthenogenesis."

"Partheno-what?"

"Parthenogenesis — it's from the Greek, meaning virgin creation. It means some species don't need a male. It's been seen in a few types of spiders, scorpions, fish, reptiles, even birds. The female may lay an already fertilized egg, or might have both male and female sex organs and handles the duties all by herself."

"Convenient."

"Tell me about it. But don't worry, Carter, the human female still needs a human male to do more than open tight pickle jar lids and kill the occasional spider."

"I wasn't saying anything," I said.

"No, but you were thinking it."

"Back to the point: As you suggested, this creature may not need a partner to reproduce. And it may be doing so right now."

"Purely speculation at this point. If it molted, as you say ticks do, the techs didn't find any evidence of it in the materials from the nest. It might still be in the nymph stage — assuming that's what we're dealing with."

"It might need a larger food source next time if it's going to be producing eggs," I said.

"A larger food source," she repeated. "More than five people?"

"Maybe five adults, maybe more. But will it want them all in one place, or dine out round-robin? You know, like a progressive dinner, with each course at a different home."

"There's a greater chance of being discovered, as well as of not being ensured a reliable food supply," she said. "And it depends, again, on whether this is a thinking hunter, or something acting on instinct."

"Possibilities ... let's see. It would need to be someplace where people go in and stay and aren't expected to come out again right away; a place without aggressive supervision, which would leave out jails, hospitals and homeless shelters. A group home perhaps; not a nursing home, though, or a day care center, because those would have too much traffic, too. Same with a church or a business," I mused.

"Is there a group home near you?"

"Lady, I just moved here," I said, lightly. "I don't get out much, either. You would probably be in a better position to find that out, even if you are in D.C. and not here."

"Gotcha," she said.

I told her I was fine with the house, despite its sordid history. I should have asked her who had the house before it was turned into a meth lab.

Heck, I should have asked her to be transferred somewhere else, right away, and let the authorities deal with this matter.

Shoulda, coulda, woulda: a description of the path not taken.

CHAPTER 17: THE FIRE

Fred and I got a little sleep after that. It was good to have a plan, even if the plan was only hinted at and not fully formed. That part could come later.

The next morning, we followed our usual — although new — routine, strolling downtown and sitting at our favorite sidewalk café. I flirted with the waitress and Fred flirted with everyone. He was better at it than I was. His collar looked better on him than my itchy beard did on me, but that's no excuse.

I picked up a newspaper someone had left behind, and suddenly had no appetite.

There it was, in a screaming headline across the top of the front page: GROUP HOME TRAGEDY

A home for people with developmental disabilities burned down in the early evening the day before, early enough to make the newspaper's deadlines. No known survivors among the seven residents and their one live-in supervisor/counselor.

Coincidence? Or did the creature know how to start fires to hide what it had done?

Can a forensic pathologist determine whether a person's blood was drained from their body if what he has is someone who was burned to a crisp? I supposed it would depend on the severity of the fire, how hot it burned and the condition of the body. Cremation pretty much hides everything, if all you have to identify a person with is a tooth or charred piece of jaw bone.

But if the body has come through the fire with much less damage, the pathologist would be able to determine all sorts of things about the victim: still breathing or already dead at the time of the fire; status of flesh on the throat; whether there was blood still in the body.

The story didn't say how bad the fire was and didn't identify the victims other than by their place of residence. Of course, there isn't much that can be found out to fill the story when the fatal fire takes place right at deadline.

I waited until Fred and I were at home again before I called Penny. She hadn't heard about it yet, so I read to her what was in the newspaper.

"Well, hell!" she said when I finished.

"Do you want me to —"

"I want you to stay at home and avoid getting involved," she snapped. Then, in a more conciliatory tone of voice: "Look, things may be about to come to a head here in your case. I don't want to have to worry about you being exposed and blowing the whole thing apart, all because of some giant tick on a rampage on the [redacted] coast. Let the local authorities do their jobs, while we do our jobs and you stay safe and undetected, all right?"

"But this thing —"

"I said, 'All right?'"

"Yes, Marshal. Fred and I will continue to lie low."

But she knew we wouldn't. We couldn't, and we definitely shouldn't. It was the path we were on, like it or not.

CHAPTER 18: THE VICTIMS

Fred and I watched the local news broadcast that day, and made certain we were in front of the TV the following days to catch the latest on the tragedy at the group home. We also picked up copies of the newspaper while on our morning strolls — the printed stories may not have been as timely as the TV reports, but they carried greater depth about what happened. Or what the authorities said had happened.

No mention was made of throat wounds or massive loss of blood. Some of the victims died of smoke inhalation. For others, the damage was too great to be able to say with certainty.

The cause of the fire was written down as a gas leak under the floor, in the building's crawlspace. The flooring throughout the house ignited about the same time and burned upward, pretty much gutting the structure.

The newspaper carried short sketches about each victim, describing their achievements as they had overcome adversity, striving to live on their own without having to be housed in a soul-deadening institution. What they had done was inspirational.

It made me sick.

It was bad enough when a family was slaughtered in their sleep, their innocence destroyed in an orgy of bloodletting. But for the group home residents to die this way, after struggling all their lives and making headway against an unforgiving society that couldn't help but push back against anyone not considered "normal," that just ate at me.

I may not have felt that empathic about fellow human beings once upon a time, but that was before Fred entered my life and made me more human.

"Fred, you know what Penny said, but we have to do something," I said.

"Yeh!" He wagged his tail.

"This thing has consumed the blood of as many as eight grown adults. I have to believe that means it intends to reproduce. We don't need more of these things hatching out, or whatever, and feeding off our most vulnerable citizens."

He tilted his head, as if he couldn't believe what I had just said.

"I sounded like a politician, didn't I?" I said. "'Vulnerable citizens.'"

"Yeh!"

"Too much TV news, I guess. OK, what do you think we should do?"

He stared at me a moment, then darted out of the room, returning shortly with the leash in his mouth.

I grinned at him as he grinned back. "Yeah, let's go hunting."

Although it was broad daylight outside, I brought along the tactical flashlight. The creature wouldn't be outdoors soaking in the sun's rays; it would be hidden away somewhere dark, where it was least likely to be discovered, as it did whatever it was going to do after having feasted on the blood of eight people.

I also carried a kitchen knife, taped to my leg. I wondered if I needed a wooden stake, then discarded the notion. Fiction required a wooden stake or something made of silver, but this was reality. OK, my reality if you're still not a believer.

In any case, I figured the creature would still be gorged with blood, and if I could rip it open and let it bleed out, that would do considerable damage even if it didn't kill it. No doubt it would set back whatever plans the creature had for all the blood it had taken.

I wished I had a gun.

I wished I had an army.

I wished I had Buffy the Vampire Slayer.

I had Fred. He was enough.

CHAPTER 19: ON PATROL

Fred and I began patrolling, first our neighborhood, then surrounding neighborhoods.

It brought to mind a movie I had seen on late-night TV when I was much younger, *The Omega Man,* starring Charlton Heston as Robert Neville. He was the sole healthy survivor of biological warfare that wiped out most of humanity and turned nearly every other survivor into a revenant who shunned the daylight and followed the ravings of a cult leader named Matthias, played by Anthony Zerbe. "Speedy Bob Neville" would jog through the empty city, looking for nests of revenants, and when he found them he'd blow them away with a machine gun or other weapon.

They weren't the vampires of the movie *The Last Man on Earth,* with Vincent Price, nor of *I Am Legend,* with Will Smith, although all three films were based on Richard Matheson's novel, also titled *I Am Legend.* It's just that I mentally flashed on the scene with Heston's character as he was pausing while jogging to make notes into a recorder, indicating his progress in clearing one building after another.

That's what Fred and I did, mapping the city in concentric circles — on a square grid, of course, since that's the way the streets lay — with our house in the center. We came across the burned group home on our third day of hunting.

Fred said the scent of the creature, if it had been there, was long gone, covered up by the still powerful odor left by the fire.

That night, as we went over the map again, marking our progress, I realized how stupid I'd been.

"I can't believe I was so stupid!" I told Fred. He didn't disagree.

We had assumed that the creature had attacked the group home and, so far, had no reason to doubt that assumption. So why were we searching concentric rings around my house?

The creature had gone from our neighborhood to the group home, and since that was the last place we believed it had been, that's where we should have begun our search.

Instead, we'd lost three days already! (Not to mention the time it took for us to realize we should be hunting this thing after the group home had burned down.)

Stupid, Carter (like Fred, it's not my original name)! Stupid!

Fred jumped up and licked me on the face until I started laughing.

"OK, let's start over," I said, studying the map.

I drew a line from our house to the eighth house down the street, then from there to the ruined group home. It wasn't a straight line, but there was a definite trend in the direction the creature was traveling.

"Now if I were a vampire of legend — or just some sort of mutated tick — where would I go to have my blood-sucking babies? Where would be the best place for thousands of hatchlings to come out and find their first meal?"

Fred watched me closely, tilting his head slightly to one side as he listened, looking a lot like the RCA Victor dog in the old ads. You know: "His master's voice."

"OK, I would be looking for — what did I call them? 'Vulnerable citizens'? Yeah, and if there are thousands of hatchlings out hunting for blood donors, Mama would no longer be concerned about keeping their presence a secret. What was it Stalin supposedly said? Oh, yeah: When one man dies it's a tragedy, but when millions die it's a statistic.

"Mama could lose 99 percent of her offspring and still have enough survivors to keep the species going. So she isn't going to be looking for an abandoned mill or isolated farmhouse. She's looking for a school or a hospital, or a jail," I told Fred. "Something where her babies would find plenty of victims unable to fight back, overwhelmed by the swarm."

"Nuh!" Fred said.

"No?"

He jumped down and crisscrossed the room, looking in one place, then another. It was clear to me that he was trying to find some way to express his thoughts, when his vocabulary wasn't quite up to the task.

Fred ran out of the room, and a short time later came back dragging a laundry basket.

"Mama's going to a Laundromat?" I asked.

He growled at me, as if to say don't be a fool, then took the laundry basket and flipped it over on himself, so that he was inside it, under it, like a dog in a cage.

In a cage, I told myself. I looked at the map. What is in a cage that is in this direction? Dogs in a kennel ... doggy day care ... too confined, closely monitored. Hmm ... no feedlot ... no, there it is!

"The zoo!" I said, and Fred barked, throwing the laundry basket off and jumping onto my lap.

"Of course! Mama may not care if her babies are discovered after they've been feeding, but she wants to give them the best chance for survival regardless. And animals in the zoo would be even more vulnerable than school kids, patients or inmates."

Fred huffed, then licked my face again.

"Yeah, Fred, you said it better than I did. And in fewer words."

That was Fred. He could speak for the voiceless.

CHAPTER 20: BIG GAME HUNT

Should I have called Penny? Things might have turned out differently if I had.

Or not. Who's to say?

Fred and I went to the zoo. On our own.

A zoo normally will not allow dogs onto the grounds. An exception is a service dog, such as one trained to work with a blind person. Another exception is a therapy dog, which is trained to help a person cope with stressful changes in his or her environment.

Fred was licensed as a therapy dog, thanks to the U.S. Marshals Service. You see, I was serious about not being separated from him, especially in those places where other dogs aren't allowed. I guess you might say he really was my therapy dog. He made me more human.

Fred and I stopped in at Guest Relations, and I assured them that he was a service animal. Asked what he was trained to do, I told them I was subject to seizures, and he was able to notice when a seizure was coming on and by alerting me would help me avoid it.

It wasn't true, but it was what the U.S. Marshals Service had recommended, and Fred had even gone through the training.

He aced it, of course. I just didn't have seizures.

The kind woman at Guest Relations radioed zoo security with a description of Fred and me, so we wouldn't be hassled during our visit. This place was growing on me already.

We entered the zoo together and he stayed close to me. As with most well-trained service animals, he ignored the zoo's distractions and remained focused on me — or so it would appear to anyone observing us. We weren't allowed in any area where he could come in direct contact with another animal, such as the children's petting area, but he otherwise had full range of the zoo grounds.

I knew Fred was scanning our surroundings as we wandered deeper and deeper into the sprawling zoological complex.

The last time I had been at a zoo, it was a disheartening visit, seeing bears and lions and tigers and all of the other animals in habitats that were little better than primitive jail cells. The elephants, at the time, were chained down with a manacle around a leg — or perhaps I'm remembering a circus of old — happily, the circuses have been eliminating elephants from their shows or on the other hand, sadly, shutting down completely.

Regardless, this zoo was worlds away from the memories that had me avoiding zoos for so long. The lion habitat looked like a savannah, while the apes lived in a small local version of a tropical jungle. It was still a sad statement about humankind's treatment of wild animals, since these creatures were born and lived and would die in captivity, but at least efforts had been made to improve their living conditions.

Fred and I went through the big cats, then the big apes, then moved on to the elephants. It took a couple of hours just to cover those areas. I checked the map that had been provided with entry and the trails through the habitats looked like a maze. There were loops and dead ends, and open areas with no apparent habitats.

We stopped at a water fountain where we both got a drink, then I sat down with Fred and described the map to him.

"I'm not sure how we can do this, Fred. This is a huge place, with lots of possible hiding places."

He looked around, saw no one in the vicinity, then dropped down and covered his eyes with his front leg.

"Darkness," I said. "The creature needs darkness. And someplace where its stink wouldn't be noticed."

"Yeh!"

I checked the map and saw an exhibit called a Nocturnal Barn. "OK, we'll try that one."

We had to backtrack past the elephants, the apes and the big cats, then swing past zebras, giraffes and okapi, until we reached the Nocturnal Barn.

It did look like a barn, and it had an open doorway under the sign "Entrance."

We walked in, turned a corner, turned another corner, and without having closed a door were suddenly in a darkness that reminded me of the Anderson place eight houses down from my own. In front of us, after my eyes adjusted to the gloom, I made out the pale shape of a wooden door. I opened it and we went in.

We were in a large room with subdued lighting. A large enclosure immediately inside housed several hundred fruit bats, flying back and forth, up and down. If they were squeaking, Fred likely could hear them, but they were silent for me, except for the fluttering of their leathery wings. Small habitats lining the outer wall held owls, snakes and other creatures more comfortable in the dark than in the daylight.

"Anything, Fred?" I whispered.

"Nuh," he responded, also quietly.

The place was dark, all right, but it was kept clean and the natural odors of the ordinary occupants were at a minimum. I certainly didn't smell the creature we were hunting, and if it had managed to hide its scent from me, even Fred didn't detect it.

We moved on.

We saw rhinos, bison, elk and grizzlies. We saw flamingos and a bald eagle, alligators and otters, a buzzard and chimpanzees.

Deer and gazelle, cranes and pheasants, swamp hogs and wild African dogs, turtles, tortoises and terrapins, but we didn't pick up any obvious sign of the bloodsucking creature we hunted.

Fred and I found another secluded park bench and had another talk.

"Could we have been wrong, Fred? Should we be checking the schools and hospitals and jails?"

"Nuh!" he said. "Heah."

"It's here somewhere?"

"Yeh!"

"So you've smelled it, here and there, but were not able to pinpoint where it is?"

"Yeh!"

I studied the map again, tracing with my finger the route we'd followed on our hunt through the zoo.

"Was there any place where the smell seemed stronger?"

"Yeh," he said. "Cass." He made the word sound like an insult.

"The cat habitats?"

"Yeh!"

I studied him. "You sure it wasn't just the cats?" That's one way Fred was like all the other dogs — he and cats did not get along.

He just looked at me, then shook all over as if he'd gotten wet and was throwing the water off, and jumped off the bench.

I had the leash in my hand, but again he was leading me.

CHAPTER 21: CLOSING IN

We backtracked across the zoo grounds. I was beginning to wonder if I should have paid for the all-day pass for the tram that rumbled through periodically, then decided if Fred could take it, so could I. After all, he had four legs, each of them quite a bit shorter than my two legs, so he had to go multiple paces for each of my strides.

We both probably would be sore tomorrow.

Heck, I was getting sore already. It was a good thing we'd been doing our daily walks and had improved our stamina.

But those walks weren't this prolonged or this stressful. We normally made lots of stops, and sat down a lot, and enjoyed relaxing at the sidewalk café.

My understanding is that everyone gets old. It's a day to day process. I just don't like that it's been happening to me while I've been busy concentrating on living forever. Sneaking up on me while my attention was focused elsewhere. You know.

We reached the cat habitats. Lions were on the left, tigers were on the right, ocelots and jaguars were straight ahead.

But what about the bloodsucking leech on two legs? (Was it two legs? Really? Not four, or six, or eight? I know I saw something that resembled the character in *Nosferatu*, but that was a face and claws. The way it slammed into me in the dark, it just as easily could have been a pit bull-size centaur with fangs.)

Fred and I checked each habitat. The cats were out, sunning themselves and ignoring — or pretending to ignore — the oh-so-easy prey on the other side of the fence as we went by. I could tell by the swishing tails and the ears that turned like radar antennas to follow our route that they were quite aware of us, or of Fred, the somewhat diminutive descendant of the wolves that once competed with their feline ancestors for prey.

Surely, I thought, if the creature had been in their pens, they would have responded, and if it had been recently, they would have been agitated. Surely.

Then again, maybe not. They're cats, after all.

I'd had cats as pets off and on while growing up. And I remember spider eggs hatching, revealing hundreds of hungry eight-legged creatures that devoured their mother before going on and seeking other prey. The cats never paid attention to the spiders, unless they did something foolish like swing on a web in front of a cat's face.

These big cats may not have recognized the stink monster as anything other than the originator of a foul odor.

Fred came to attention in front of a cat habitat bearing a sign that read, "EXHIBIT TEMPORARILY EMPTY."

I studied the empty pen, noting the open stone that a cat could sun itself on, a grassy area, tree limbs for climbing, and a cave the cat could retreat into for sleeping or whatever. A dark, protected, secluded place in the uninhabited habitat and, it turns out, the perfect place for a light-wary creature to lay her eggs.

Fred shucked his collar and attached leash like a professional escape artist, and in a moment had found a way into the pen that the zoo personnel somehow had missed or overlooked. I didn't even see how he got in; just that he had.

He approached the cave, paused, sneezed, then looked at me. I nodded and he went in.

CHAPTER 22: MISTAKES WERE MADE

It was at this point, I think, that I really began to regret not calling U.S. Marshal Penny Ransome.

She with the oddly ironic name: Penny Ransome. I couldn't help but smile remembering that day a year or so earlier when she told me her name. "Don't short-change yourself, Marshal. If you were being ransomed, I'm sure it would be for a lot more than just a penny."

Talk about getting off on the wrong foot. I should have known that was probably ranked among the top worst things I could have said to this unsmiling law enforcement officer who was taking me into custody.

"Is my foot bleeding? I think I just shot myself there," I said, as she handcuffed me. She wasn't gentle about it, either.

Months later we were able to laugh over it, but at the time it just wasn't funny. I had, after all, just confessed to knowing where a body was buried — a body that, indeed, had been buried by me.

I hadn't confessed to the local police, nor to the sheriff, not even to the state investigative bureau and most definitely not to the FBI or the DEA. No, I'd waited until I'd met this U.S. Marshal, a stout black woman who was maybe a decade older than me, and I couldn't keep my mouth shut any longer.

Don't get me wrong. This isn't one of those stories you read where the dashing, handsome hero meets up with the amazing, beautiful law enforcement officer, wins her over and they go on crazy adventures or follow esoteric clues on worldwide scavenger hunts to further the plot along and, sooner or later, end up in bed together.

Sorry if this disappoints.

I'm sure Penny Ransome could be beautiful if she applied herself, spent an ungodly amount of time with a hair stylist and beautician and chose the perfect outfit. In fact, I know she can, because I've seen the wedding photos. She was radiant on the day she gave up her maiden name for a man named Jake and became a Ransome.

But as I said, there was an age difference, plus that marital thing, and while on the job she looks rather plain and, as for me, well, my days of being movie star gorgeous never escaped their daydream status.

Strictly business between the marshal and me, that business including a jail cell and, later, a safe house when it became clear to the U.S. Attorney that I was more valuable as a witness than as a notch on a judge's gavel.

My wife and I never had children, when we were married, and I'd like to think if we had, they might have grown up to be like Penny.

She has an innate ability to gain a person's confidence and get them to open up, much as I had. She would have been able to convince the staff at the zoo that it was in their best interests to let Fred and me explore the grounds. Surely.

But I hadn't called her. Fred and I went off on our own. And we drew attention to ourselves, unwittingly.

CHAPTER 23: BUSTED

We'd forgotten, or just had overlooked, the closed circuit television cameras that were everywhere at the zoo. No, scratch that. I had forgotten the ever-present cameras. Fred didn't care. And I should have known better.

Even though the pen was an empty habitat, that didn't mean that the zoo wasn't keeping an eye on it anyway.

Fred was backing out of the cat cave, dragging what looked like an egg without a shell, about the size of half a loaf of artisanal bread. As soon as the thing was exposed to sunlight, it began to pop and sizzle like a chicken egg that had been dropped onto a hot griddle.

At the same time, two security guards walked up.

Fred and I were busted.

CHAPTER 24: EXPELLED

I was lucky. I guess.

Fred and I were escorted to Guest Relations, where they made a photocopy of my I.D. and took a photo of me, then we were escorted out of the zoo to my car, where they made a note of its make and model, plus the license plate, and informed me that I was no longer welcome at the zoo and if they ever caught me there again, I would be arrested for trespassing and any other complaints they could think of to lodge against me.

I thanked them for their courtesy and professionalism, added that whatever they earned they weren't paid enough, then Fred and I returned home without saying anything further.

Wallowing in our embarrassment, I suppose.

Once home, however, we returned to the topic foremost on our minds.

"That one egg was all you found?" I asked Fred.

"Yeh."

"We covered the entire zoo, or as much as we could, and that was the only thing we could find."

"Yeh."

"Something isn't right here."

He just stared at me for a moment, then went into the kitchen for a drink of water and a snack. Clearly, thinking about it would be my job.

So I sat there, trying to figure out how we could have been so wrong about the zoo.

But were we wrong? Really?

As it turned out, Fred did find traces of the creature at the zoo. He did detect its odor, and when he went into the cat habitat, he came out with what looked like an egg — one which reacted rather badly to exposure to the light.

Was that a single egg, or a cluster of eggs? Knowing nothing about the creature itself, or how it would reproduce, I had no way of knowing whether this was a victory or a minor setback.

One egg? A cluster of eggs? Hard to say when the evidence burns up as it is exposed to daylight, and then you're expelled from the zoo.

I shrugged. When in doubt, do as Fred does. I got up and went into the kitchen to make myself a sandwich.

Afterward, I lay down on the couch, Fred nestled in his usual position, and we both drifted off for a short nap. Our adventure at the zoo had proven tiring.

The "short nap" lasted the night. Our day at the zoo had been more exhausting than I'd realized. And the couch proved to be rather comfortable. It didn't even bother us that we were asleep in front of the fireplace.

Fred and I were awakened long before we were ready the next morning when the doorbell rang.

CHAPTER 25: INTERROGATION

Unlike other dogs, Fred doesn't bark when someone rings the doorbell. That's one of the many things I love about him.

I looked out through the peephole in the door. Standing on the other side was a woman in uniform.

A zoo uniform.

Uh-oh.

I opened the door.

"Mr. Carter? Do you mind if I come in?" She was a tall brunette, easy on the eye with a tan that indicated she spent a lot of time outdoors.

"Am I in trouble? I mean, more than I already am?"

"Not as far as I'm concerned," she said. "I just have some questions about what happened yesterday."

Yesterday? I noticed the position of the sun, and checked my watch. About 9:30 a.m. It was tomorrow, already.

Well, I had questions, too. I invited her in.

Fred wagged his tail. That was a good sign, I thought.

We went into the living room. She took a seat. I asked if she'd like something to drink — I had sun tea I'd started yesterday before going to the zoo — and she accepted. When I returned with two glasses of iced tea, I found Fred in her lap, accepting a belly rub.

Definitely a good sign.

"What can I do for you, ah, Miss ...?" No ring on her finger.

"Julie Evans," she said. "I'm a researcher at the zoo, specializing in the big cats."

"Nice to meet you, Miss Evans," I said. "What can I do for you?"

"Something strange happened yesterday involving you and this little guy," she said, now scratching Fred's head behind his ears.

"That's Fred," I said.

"Hi, Fred," she said, and he sighed. Sucker for a woman in uniform who's good with her hands, I thought.

She looked at me, locked her eyes with mine, and said, "What happened? What did you do?"

Brown eyes, in a tanned face with no apparent makeup, under brown hair. They bored into me as if she could read my soul.

I played the innocent. "What do you mean?"

She rolled her eyes, chucked Fred under the chin one last time and set him down on the floor, then leaned forward and pierced me with those eyes again.

"Mr. Carter, as you know, we have cameras all over the zoo. I've spent last night watching recordings of you roaming the zoo, apparently aimlessly, paying little attention to the animals, until suddenly you make a bee line across the grounds to the cat habitat. Once there, your dog, Fred, shucks his collar and enters an unoccupied pen in some way that we still haven't been able to make out, then comes out of the cat's den dragging something the size of an ostrich egg that ends up looking like a fried omelet."

So much for trying to stay under the radar. Fred and I left records all over the place, it appeared. The U.S. Marshal would not be pleased at all.

So I leaned forward in return. "You say I'm not in trouble."

"No more than already."

"And you just want answers."

"Yes."

"You may not like the answers."

"Try me."

I thought about it. What was the worst that could happen if I told her the truth? She'd decide I was a lunatic and beat a hasty retreat. I was already banned from the zoo; they couldn't double-ban me.

On the other hand, if she did believe me, I might gain an ally in this battle. A local ally, that is. I already had a U.S. Marshal on my side, sort of, but she was miles away.

Miss Evans was easy on the eye. And Fred liked her.

That was the key: Fred liked her. He could read people like I read books. Of course, Fred was a dog, with thousands of generations of experience in dealing with the best and the worst of humanity, as competition, as companion, as collaborator, as best friend when no one else cares.

So I told her. Not all of it, of course. I left out Fred's ability to talk to me — that was up to him to reveal, not me — and besides, it would make my story that much harder to believe unless he wanted to speak up for himself.

Nor did I say anything about being in the program. As far as Miss Evans was concerned, I was just a single man of indeterminate income living here with my dog, of my own free will.

But I told her about the nest under the house, about how Fred and I discovered the nest thanks to his sense of smell and my curiosity about what he was so interested in beneath the fireplace.

Then I told her about the family down the street, supposedly dying of carbon monoxide poisoning. I lied about my role in the discovery, and said I had witnessed the victims myself when I entered with the other neighbors.

"To call it carbon monoxide poisoning when it's obvious someone's throat has been ripped open is just plain bizarre," I said, "but if that's the official line I'm not going to publicly speak out against it."

Next, I told her about the group home.

"Did you see those bodies, too?" she asked.

"No."

"Then what makes you think they were victims of this 'vampire-like creature'?" The quotes she put around the term were quite audible, if unspoken.

"I have no evidence," I admitted. "At least nothing that would hold up in a court of law." I scratched my beard. "I don't have access to the autopsies and haven't spoken with the firefighters or police officers who were at the scene. It all may be a result of my fevered imagination, and it wouldn't surprise me if you didn't believe me. But this is all part of the reasoning that led me to the zoo."

"OK, go on," she said, leaning back and crossing her arms. Clearly reserving judgment, and not necessarily inclined in my favor, at that.

"I figured, as with the house down the street, the authorities would cover up the true cause of these deaths as well. They don't want to stir up the community if they don't have to, especially if they don't understand what is actually going on."

"But you do." It wasn't a question, but it wasn't a challenge, either.

"I have my suspicions."

I explained my reasoning — the creature's first reaction to the dim penlight under my house, the darkened house down the street and, I presumed, the group home while under cover of darkness — that it was trying to avoid the light. Then I referred to ticks and their practice of gorging themselves on blood, molting into the next phase of development, gorging again and then reproducing.

"I don't understand, Mr. Carter. Are you calling this a vampire? Or a giant tick?" A question, true, but disbelief still hovered in the background, watching closely.

I smiled. "My problem exactly, Miss Evans. I've discounted the legends of vampires as just that: legends. There may be a basis of truth behind the legends, but what fiction has given us is just a lot of fiction. I don't buy that this thing is a Dracula or some other former human being that has been transformed into a creature of the night, nor do I think it is an insect or arachnid, or whatever, that has naturally mutated into a giant.

"Until I lay my hands on it, or get it into the hands of an expert, I'm reserving judgment about what it is. I'm just going by what it does, which is to tear into the throats of its victims, suck the blood out of their bodies and, if given enough time, apparently cover up what it has done to throw off any pursuit."

"Except for you," she said.

"Yes, I guess I am pursuing it," I admitted.

"So what led you to the zoo?" This was indeed a question. Was I winning my case before Judge Julie? Her arms uncrossed, and she leaned forward again.

I continued to explain my reasoning, how I had discounted schools, hospitals and jails as possible breeding targets, while the zoo would be a much safer option for the thing I was imagining. "This creature wouldn't know about the video cameras at the zoo," I said. "Heck, I forgot about them myself!

"But what better place to lie low, reproduce in safety, and have plenty of food supply for the babies when they hatch out at the same time? An elephant could probably feed dozens of them at once. By the time anyone in authority became aware of what was happening, they would be in hiding again, waiting for their next chance to feed."

She nodded. "Supposing you are right about everything else, that makes sense." Good, she was starting to see it from my point of view.

"So Fred and I went to the zoo to see if we could track this thing down," I said. "That's a lot of ground to cover, which is why it looked like we were roaming everywhere. But it was at the cat habitats that Fred had the strongest response. That's why we went back there."

"Fred had the 'strongest response?'" she said. Had I lost the argument before Judge Julie?

"He has the nose," I said, trying to cover up my slip. You're not supposed to be able to communicate that clearly with a "normal" dog. "He sneezes when he smells this thing."

"Might he not sneeze at the big cats? Lions and tigers, for instance, are not odorless."

"No argument there," I said. "I wondered about it myself, didn't I, Fred?" I picked him up and hugged him. He squirmed loose, jumped down, glared at me a moment and shook himself much as he had the day before at the zoo, then went into the kitchen where I could hear him lapping up another drink. He knew what I was saying, and was insulted.

"Anyway," I continued, "Fred ignored the big cats. He went to the unoccupied pen — which makes sense if you're looking for a creature that doesn't want to be discovered. How he got in, I couldn't tell you — it surprised me as much as it did you — and that thing he pulled out, well, I'm no expert but I'd wager whatever it was didn't belong there."

"An egg sac," she said.

"You said it; I didn't."

She nodded. "That might explain what I saw in the video."

"Did you get a close look at it in the pen?"

"No. It was nothing more than a stain on the rock when I went in to look at it."

"Supposing I am correct about this, would you consider that to be a survival trait?"

"How do you mean?"

"Say ... this thing is like the vampire of legend and can't survive exposure to daylight. Ultraviolet light, perhaps; I don't know. Its continued existence depends on not being discovered by this world's most fearsome predator — us. That means even its eggs, if they die when exposed to sunlight, would have to disappear before being collected as evidence of this thing's existence." I was thinking aloud here. "Discounting the development of forensic science, which goes beyond evolutionary status, to the average observer there is no connection between a smear on the rock and the eggs of a bloodsucking monster."

"In other words," she said, "a survival trait."

"Exactly!"

"All right, then, assuming you are correct about everything, we have a problem," she said. Had I won my case? She continued: "But I can tell you, without any uncertainty, that you are not."

"'Not'?"

"Not correct about everything."

CHAPTER 26: WHAT I MISSED

In my life, I have been wrong about countless things. It goes with living. Nobody is perfect. Nobody is above making the wrong decisions now and then — for some people, it's more a case of a wrong decision now and again, and again, every time.

In my old life, I had trusted my neighbors, trusted my coworkers, heck, even trusted family members, and what did it get me? A contract on my life, a chance to do quality time behind bars, and an opportunity to start over again a thousand miles away, without friends or family for support.

But I knew I wasn't wrong about this thing that was ripping out throats and draining the blood from its victims. And Fred and I had found an egg sac from this thing at the zoo. I was absolutely certain about it.

Miss Evans, however, was a researcher at the zoo who knew a thing or two more about wildlife than I would ever be able to learn on my own.

"What did I miss?"

She stood up and started to pace. I noticed Fred had come back into the room and was watching her closely.

"To be clear," she said, "I have not bought into your vampire theory all the way. I still have my doubts — at say about 20 percent — which still gives me reason to take your suppositions as possible and to draw inferences from them."

I loved the way she talked.

"What you missed, Mr. Carter, is that the zoo is only part of the entire zoological park."

"I don't follow."

"We have been expanding the park, bit by bit, over the years, adding the special elephant habitat, and expanding the great apes' and the lions' habitats. Where do you think we've gotten the land for expansion?"

It dawned on me then. "You have a lot of undeveloped land, or land that is being shaped and developed but isn't open to the public yet."

"On the nose, Mr. Carter," she said, tapping her nose. "On the nose."

"So it would make more sense for this creature to nest someplace where people don't go, but is close to the zoo grounds so the babies would have access to easy prey," I surmised aloud.

"Not only that, but I think I know where it would go, if it's there," she said. "If it exists."

She smiled at me then. "I didn't say that. I don't know whether it exists or not, but I can see you believe it. If there is any risk there to my cats, I need to look into it. Would you like to come?"

"I've ... ah ... been banished from the zoo," I reminded her.

"You'll be with me, and we'll be on the grounds where the zoo proper still hasn't reached."

Fred barked.

"Is it OK to bring Fred along?"

She kneeled in front of Fred and ruffled the hair on his head. "Will you behave, Fred?"

"Yeh!" he said.

She may not have recognized it as a word, but I did. I winked at Fred and he left the room, returning momentarily with the leash in his mouth.

"That's a smart dog," she said.

"So he keeps telling me," I said with a grin.

CHAPTER 27: CITY WILDERNESS

Access to the wilderness area adjacent to the zoo grounds was on the far end from the zoo, which made sense. It didn't appear to have any connection to the zoo, wasn't in a developed area — yet — and had a stream running through it, which also would put a damper on alternative development plans.

It was a rugged area, with wooded hills and hidden drop-offs, she told me. It would take years of effort and tens of millions of dollars, if not more, to make it safe for the average zoo guest to be able to stroll through it safely while observing the antics of young chimpanzees at play, or rare reptiles sunning themselves in their own habitat.

We left the developed areas and rumbled down a poorly maintained road surrounded by woods. I had no idea anything like this could still exist inside a city that had been here for such a long time. She told me this was once rural land, but had been encompassed by an expanding city limits decades ago as developments went up around it and residents clamored for city services. The owner of this land had left it to the city in his will for the purposes of expanding the zoo, and the city had bowed to his wishes and left it undeveloped.

"Oh, no!" she said, as she pulled her car to a halt beside what looked like a trail into the wooded area.

"What?"

"I forgot!" she said. "Sometimes there's a homeless camp back in here."

"A homeless camp! How many?"

"It depends. Sometimes just two or three, once there were as many as 30 when security rousted them out."

I muttered a few choice words as we all exited the car and faced the woods. Fred started pulling at the leash. Something, or someone, was in there.

He sneezed.

CHAPTER 28: MORE VICTIMS

Fred led the way, followed by me, of course, since I had the other end of the leash in hand, then Miss Evans. The trail through the brush and timber was fairly clear, and even to my eyes had definitely been used by a lot of people, not that long ago. The litter was a clear sign. Fast food bags and wrappers, soft drink containers, dirty disposable diapers, empty plastic cell phone packages, orange rinds and egg shells — if it could be found in your trash at home it could be found here as well. I also noticed packages that once had held meat, just like what was found under my house.

Fred came to a branch in the trail and paused, sniffing in one direction, then sniffing the other. He looked back at me.

I turned to Miss Evans. "How familiar are you with this area? Which way leads to the homeless camp?"

"The trail on the left. The one on the right goes toward the bluff, where there is an unofficial swimming area with a waterfall."

We took the trail more traveled, and soon could see tents set up in a clearing ahead.

Just tents. Red tents, orange tents, brown tents, blue tents. No people.

"Would they hide if they heard us coming?"

"No," she said. "Not for just a couple of people. If we were a security squad, or the police, then yes, they'd scatter."

"You might want to stay here," I said.

"No way, Mr. Carter. I'm coming with you!"

We approached the camp, making plenty of noise.

"Hello, the camp!" I called. "Anyone there?"

It was silent. I counted a dozen tents, some of them the cheap pup tents you could get at a surplus store, others pop-up affairs that could hold a family of six, and two that consisted of tarps spread across cords stretched between trees.

It also reeked. Unwashed bodies, open toilets, spilled alcohol and lots of decaying flesh.

Miss Evans turned away and vomited. I managed to hold mine down, but it wasn't easy.

"Fred, is anyone still alive?"

I released him from the leash and he ran through the small tent city, checking each one before returning and huffing, "Nuh!"

I turned to Miss Evans, expecting her to still be incapacitated, but she was standing beside me, wiping her mouth while staring at Fred in disbelief.

"Did he say ...?"

"My Fred is an intelligent guy, Miss Evans, but you know a dog's mouth isn't shaped to be able to speak words, right?"

She looked at me, then looked at Fred again, then shook her head. I heard, "Can't be," under her breath.

Then, "We need to call the police."

"And do what? Turn ourselves in?" I said. "We are the only ones with any inkling of what is going on here. We need to find this thing and destroy it — then we can call in the authorities and show them the corpse of the creature that killed these people. They may still deny their own eyes, but at least it gives us something to point at when we're on trial for mass murder. Maybe we can convince a jury."

Now she stared at me in disbelief. "Are you serious?"

"Think about it the way the police might. I'm already on record at the zoo for trespassing, getting in trouble and being ejected. They have my photo and everything — make that, you have my photo and everything. Then you come to my house and we conspire to do something in the wilderness behind the zoo. Perhaps clear out a tent city of interlopers who are interfering with the zoo's expansion. Then things go bad and we kill everyone and drain the blood from their bodies, for whatever reason. I'm sure the police will be glad to come up with some sort of Stephen King-like answer. Blood sacrifice, maybe. Religious cult stuff.

"And if you want to bring up the group home and the house down the street from mine, God only knows what sort of field day they'd have with that connection."

She stood there staring at me, thinking it through. I could tell from her expression it wasn't going my way. I could tell she was wondering what I might have done last night, after I left the zoo.

"Look," I said, seeking to distract her and get her back on the right track. "When we left my house, you said you thought you knew of a likely place the creature could be hiding. I'd say this slaughter here is a pretty good indication you're correct. Where is it?"

She frowned. Then she pointed back the way we came. "The other branch of the trail," she said. "It leads to a waterfall. There are caves in the bluff above and beside the falls."

"Fred, let's go," I said. Then, to her, "And you can decide whether you want to come with us and hunt this thing, or go out and alert the police. I leave it to you."

I paused a moment, then added, "I swear to you I had nothing to do with this beyond what I've already told you. I did not kill these people."

She nodded, her expression grim. "Lead on, Mr. Carter."

CHAPTER 29: THE CAVES

Fred remained off the leash as we backtracked along the trail to the branch. I knew he wouldn't go off on his own, and I was certain he'd proven his reliability to Miss Evans back at the campsite.

The less-traveled trail led us to a stream fed eventually by a pool that was well-watered by a waterfall.

"This is nice. I'm surprised it isn't used as a swimmin' hole," I said.

"It was, until the zoo let it be known a gator might have escaped."

"Really?"

"The rumor? Yes. In reality, I ain't sayin'."

I laughed. Just being in this part of the woods, beside this beauty, was a relief after what we had witnessed moments earlier. Not that it hadn't been horrific, but the human mind has to find ways to cope, and humor in the face of death is one of those coping mechanisms. Don't judge me. Judge the situation.

The waterfall fell from about 12 feet above the pool surface, and the bluff rose on either side of the falls by perhaps another dozen feet. I noticed some odd stone outcroppings on either side of the stream at the top of the falls, looking almost like lower fangs in a jaw.

I pointed them out to Miss Evans and she said, "Stalagmites. What you're looking at is what was once an underground stream. The cave it flowed through collapsed a long, long time ago. Those are stalagmites that survived the collapse of the cave.

"If we were to climb up and walk along the streambed, we could find other examples of cave architecture, such as flowstone. The caves in the side of the hill above and beside the falls are surviving parts of the underground structure."

I laughed, and said, "That's a relief. I was afraid you were going to say the water was flowing through the lower jaw of some prehistoric monster."

"If that were the case, this would be open to the public and we'd be charging admission."

"So how do we climb up and explore the caves?"

"That's just it, Mr. Carter. We climb up. I guess Fred will just have to stay down here."

She went up to the base of the slope beside the falls. It had some slant, but was still steep, mostly solid rock with a number of cracks and outcroppings — sort of similar to a recreational climbing wall, only made by nature. She began to climb, testing her handholds before pulling herself up, then testing where she placed her feet before putting weight on them.

I pulled a forehead-carried flashlight out of my pocket and situated it onto my head, then I shrugged at Fred and chose a place slightly to the left of where she was climbing and followed suit.

Fred was not content to stay behind. I glanced back at him and saw him galloping toward the steep slope, then he leaped, hit the surface beside me and, with all four paws in gear, he raced up past Miss Evans and into what I now saw was the mouth of the first cave. He disappeared into the cave, then reappeared at the entrance and grinned down at us, barely panting from the exertion.

He wasn't sneezing. I guessed that was a good sign.

Miss Evans looked back at me.

"Yeah, he's got four on the floor, all-paw-drive," I said. "Back home, the squirrels all live in terror."

She made the cave next, then scooted over inside to give me room as I reached the entrance. It appeared to be a shallow scoop in the rocky hillside. And it did not reek of rotting blood.

"There's more up here than this," she said. "This is just the first cave that can be reached. There's another one above and to the right."

"Fred?" I said, and he jumped into my arms. "Whew! Good thing you aren't any larger or you would have knocked me over," I told him. "OK, up and to the right," I said, launching his small body up the slope above the cave entrance we crouched inside.

"It's as if he understands everything you're saying," Miss Evans said.

"He's really intelligent," I said. "I've read the average dog can understand about 165 words, but Fred knows a lot more than that."

"Seriously?"

"Sure! When he was a puppy, I used to read him to sleep. He had favorite books," I said. "Come on, he's leaving us behind."

I resumed climbing and this time she followed me.

The second cave entrance was about even with the falls, but around the side of the cliff where the moisture from the falling water didn't reach. Fred stood in the entrance, sneezing.

"Something's in there," I said.

I reached up and switched on my forehead flashlight, then climbed the rest of the way to the entrance. The smell was bad enough to gag a garbage man.

"Whew! Fred, you been eating beans and rare bear?" He huffed and turned to gaze into the darkness. The jokes I made about his farts embarrassed him. "Sorry, Fred, couldn't help it."

The cave had a low ceiling, so I couldn't stand upright, but in my crouch I was able to pull a second flashlight from my pocket and hand it to Miss Evans as she joined us. It was the same tactical flashlight I'd used in the house down the street from me.

"How far back does this go?" I asked. I could smell the rotting blood stench that the creature gave off like a skunk with a permanent on-switch. Fred was sneezing again, but made no move to retreat.

"God! What a stink!"

"That's it, or them," I said, wishing I'd thought to bring something to cover my nose. "How far?"

"Um, about 20 feet, I think. It zigs and zags and comes out just above the falls. It might have been a reliever route when the main stream became flooded, back when it was underground."

"Zigs and zags, eh? Probably gets pretty dark toward the middle."

"Very," she said.

I crept forward, following the beam of my forehead light. "Don't turn that on until you have it in your sight," I said. "Then pull the head of the flashlight out to zoom it, and it'll act like a phaser set on kill."

"Thank you, Mr. Spock," she said.

"Spock?"

"Sure. If you were more like Yoda, you would have said 'light saber.'"

"You didn't strike me as the science fiction-reading type."

"Oh? What did you think I read?"

"I don't know. *Narnia* or the *Lord of the Rings*."

"I read those too, and watch the shows."

"My apologies for the unwarranted assumption. Why call me Spock, and not Kirk?"

She laughed. "Spock is logical, like you. Kirk would have tried to get me in bed already, and probably have succeeded."

"What?"

"I have a thing for Kirk."

Fred barked, interrupting the witty repartee.

And he sneezed, several times, then growled.

CHAPTER 30: THE THING, ONLY BIGGER

The beam from my forehead flashlight caught something briefly that dodged out of sight, going farther down the cave.

"It's just up in front of us," I said, quietly.

"I saw," she said, also keeping her voice low. She switched on the flashlight but held her palm over the beam. I could see a glow passing through the back of her hand, like a soft night light. It was a bright, bright light, especially in that dark cave.

We crept forward, crouched down. I was suddenly wishing we'd stopped somewhere, a pet store perhaps, and gotten us some large leather collars like Fred's that we could have used on ourselves to protect our throats from this creature.

They might not have stopped it, but they might have slowed it down to give us a chance.

"Don't let it get close. It's fast for its size."

"How do you know that?"

I'd forgotten that I hadn't told her about the close brush I had with it inside the dead girl's bedroom.

"You just saw it move. That is no turtle in front of us."

"Tortoise," she said.

"What?"

"A tortoise is a land creature, moving slowly. A turtle lives in the water, and can be relatively fast in its element."

"Now who's being Spock?"

"I work at the zoo!"

I saw movement ahead. "There! Can you see it?"

She answered with light, blasting the cave in front of us with I've forgotten how many Lumens.

They were enough.

It was Nosferatu of sorts, all right. Pale face, fangs close together in its mouth, claws at the end of its upper arms. But it didn't look all that human. It did look pregnant, though, or well-fed. It couldn't retreat; I could see a glimmer of daylight coming from the passageway behind it. The creature shrieked.

Miss Evans concentrated the tight light beam on its swollen belly.

Suddenly it exploded, like a water balloon filled with blood.

You know what happens when a water balloon bursts, right? If there's enough water pressure inside the balloon, everything around it gets soaked.

Fred and Miss Evans and I scrambled out of the cave as fast as we could, spitting and wiping our eyes, then we skidded down the slope on our asses and flung ourselves into the pool of water below the waterfall, never mind any gators, leaving three trails of blood as we passed.

"Oh God!" Miss Evans said, ducking under water, then coming up to say "Oh God!" again.

I think I was saying something a little coarser, but with the same intent.

Fred was acting as if he enjoyed being wet for once. I rubbed at his hairy body, forcing the blood out into the fresh water.

He was the first to leave the pool, shook a lot of the water off, then lay down in the sun to keep an eye on Miss Evans and me.

"What did I tell you? Like a phaser set to kill," I said.

"What was that thing?" she said. "It wasn't human."

I helped her out of the pool, then we mutually turned our backs on each other and took off our clothing to wring the water out of the fabric. I sneaked a peek and caught her peeking at me. We grinned at each other.

"Not Kirk, huh?" I said.

"Well, I do like what I see."

"So do I. But we're both shivering, and there's a bunch of dead people on the other side of those trees. Let's get out of here."

We didn't say it, but I think it was pretty clear between us that we had no desire to climb back up and check on that thing in the cave. At least not right now. Not today. Maybe not tomorrow. Maybe never.

We dressed in our damp clothing and slogged down the path toward her car. Moments later we were soaking the seats of her car and headed home. My home.

CHAPTER 31: MORE THERE

After playing Captain Kirk and the green Orion dancing girl into the night, Julie (no longer "Miss Evans") and I lay in bed, discussing the thing we'd hunted down and zapped with killing light.

"Was that it? Is it over?" she finally asked.

Fred, who joined us in bed after the sheets stopped jumping, spoke up then. "Nuh," he said. "Moh bere."

Julie sat up then, staring at Fred.

I grinned. "I told you he was intelligent."

"You also said a dog's mouth isn't shaped right to be able to make words."

"I did say that, didn't I? But I didn't say Fred couldn't speak."

She thought for a moment, scratching Fred between the ears again. "That's what you implied. But ... oh, it wasn't your decision to reveal Fred's gift, was it?" She turned to Fred, leaned over and touched her nose to his. "It was your decision," she told him.

He licked her on the nose, and said, "Yeh!"

"Thank you, Fred. I won't violate your trust."

He wagged his tail almost hard enough to detach it, then flipped over on his back to invite her to scratch his belly, which she did.

"He knows you won't," I said. "You are only the fourth person he's trusted with this knowledge."

"So there's you and me. Who are the others?"

"The breeder who brought his parents together, and a law enforcement officer whose identity I am not allowed to divulge."

"Secrets upon secrets," she said.

"Buried on top of yet more secrets."

"Well, leaving that aside for now, we have this other, rather pressing secret. There are dead bodies on zoo property and a creature we left behind in that cave," she said.

I nodded. "My suggestion is to call zoo security and ask them to check the property and ..."

She was shaking her head no.

"No?"

"No!" she said.

"Why not?"

"I don't have any authority to send the security people anywhere. I'm just a researcher, watching the big cats at the zoo and explaining their habits to curious visitors. But what I can do is mention to someone who does have the authority that I might have seen someone walking into the woods. No muss, no fuss, and no one connects us with what they find."

"That's good," I said.

"Uh huh, but it isn't enough."

"What do you mean?"

"We got one creature."

"Yeah?"

"Fred said there are more of them."

"Yes, he did."

"Would he know that?"

I nodded. "Yes, he would. I've never known Fred to be wrong about anything."

"Then we're going to have to go back in there."

CHAPTER 32: THE OFFICIAL STORY

Julie went home about 4 a.m. to shower and get a little sleep before getting up and going in to work at the zoo. She dropped her hint, and by the time she got off work and came over to my house, the evening news was buzzing about the illness that had claimed the lives of 15 people who had been living in a tent city below the zoo.

"Hantavirus? Really?" Julie said, as we sat together watching the news in the living room.

I muted the television so we wouldn't be interrupted by inane chatter between news readers with no empathy. "It's a pretty good cover-up, considering," I said.

"Considering what?"

"Well, I'm sure you know the hantavirus is passed on essentially by breathing mouse poop."

"Or urine or saliva. Hmpf, as if someone was going to breathe a mouse's saliva!"

"Right. In any case, the official story is that these people were poor and homeless, and so they were not in the best of health to begin with. There were mice in the camp ..."

"I didn't see any."

"No, but you weren't looking for mice. Anyway, all 15 of these poor souls came into contact with mouse poop, urine or saliva, and came down with the illness about the same time."

"What a coincidence!" The sarcasm was clear.

"Yeah, how 'bout that! Anyway, it's speculated that they suffered through the fatigue, fever and muscle aches, which affected the large muscle groups. You know, the thighs, the hips, the back."

"You've been doing your homework," she said.

"They mentioned hantavirus earlier in a bulletin while you were at work and I looked it up online. All I know is what the Centers for Disease Control and Prevention tell me, and the news media. You know. Anyway, they started experiencing other symptoms, like headaches, dizziness and chills, and began throwing up and having diarrhea."

"Those symptoms could be any number of things. The flu, Legionnaire's disease, food poisoning."

"Right, which, according to the cover-up, may be why the sick people at the tent city didn't seek medical attention. They may have thought it would pass, or they were members of one of those religions that believe prayer is more effective than modern medicine.

"In any case, they didn't improve, and they began having trouble breathing as their lungs filled with fluid. Already weakened by malnutrition, they all died where they lay. No one was healthy enough to get out to seek help."

"Holy crap!" she said. "They didn't have cell phones to call for help?"

"It's a cover-up, remember? Besides, the folks covering this up have that figured out, too. Because this is all undeveloped area, in a low-lying spot, there was no cell reception there. I'm sure when the zoo expands into that region, cell towers will be added to the construction and the phones will work. But until that time, it's wilderness."

She shook her head. "You delight in this, don't you?"

"What do you mean? I think it's horrible what happened!"

"I know that! But this cover-up, it's like you own it, like you came up with it yourself."

I couldn't tell her I had experience with this sort of thing, back in my previous life. And actually admired the craftsmanship involved in coming up with the alternative story.

Could I?

Dare I?

I turned to Fred. I trusted his judgment.

He was lying in front of the fireplace, in the same spot where he lay that day he warned me about the thing under the house. He was watching us, listening.

"Fred? Should I tell her?"

He stared at me a moment, clearly thinking about what I'd asked, then he hopped up, came over and sniffed Julie's ankles. He then jumped up and sniffed her hands, and finally her face. She sat there and accepted his scrutiny without protest.

"Yeh!" he huffed. He licked her face and she hugged him.

So I began to talk.

"Fred wasn't always called Fred. My parents did not name me Earl Carter. If you tell anyone about this, Fred will die and I will die and you probably will die, too, just because you know this.

"I would do nothing to harm you, but there are people who want to do harm to me, and who would harm you as well just to get at me," I said.

She said she understood (even if she didn't, really), so I went on ...

CHAPTER 33: THE FINANCIER

My family has connections. Politicians, police, district attorneys, judges at all levels from justice of the peace to federal, funeral directors, doctors, lawyers, preachers and other crooks. Heck, we even own parts of dairies, dry cleaners, coffee shops, barbershops, city utilities, ambulance services, plumbers, electricians, massage parlors, bookstores and, until most of them went out of business, video rentals.

You see, my grandfather, when he was young, fancied himself a private banker. He would make some money, legitimately, then would invest it in things that no actual banker would touch. This private financing would involve collecting a percentage of whatever profits the business would make, off the top.

And unlike legitimate bankers, there was no paying off the debt. Once the deal was made, that was it. Income forever. Like buying a house and renting it out.

Usually it was legal. He saw himself as an off-the-books stockholder, a silent partner, buying a small share of the enterprise. He was an equal opportunity investor, financing under the table as well as over.

My grandfather became known as The Financier. Believe it or not, his rates were fair and reasonable, generally, depending on how much he invested. Sometimes it took years to recoup his investment, but once that happened, the rest was a never-ending flow of money. Free money. Unregulated by the government, coming or going.

If, say, a dry cleaner my grandfather had helped acquire his business chose to sell, the agreement had to state that the purchaser would continue making the payments to The Financier. Often, my grandfather would also be financing the purchaser, so the payments to The Financier just doubled.

He was reasonable, though. His requirements were not outrageous; he wanted any business he invested in to succeed. After all, you don't strangle the goose that is laying golden eggs. He was known to send customers their way, to help them out.

He got lots of referrals from people he did business with. When every bank would turn someone down, there was always my grandfather, willing to give the entrepreneur one more opportunity to make good on his dream. Some of them did especially well, and my grandfather got his cut of the profits.

He believed in diversification. He believed in giving people second chances, too. After all, a loss one day might turn into extra gain the next, if conditions improved.

But he also had a way of cutting his losses when it was clear that the flow of free money was being strangled. He wasn't above a baseball bat to the kneecap, or the removal of the tip of a finger without anesthesia. Like Jimmy Hoffa, the union leader who disappeared and whose body was never found, there were people my grandfather dealt with who disappeared and were never heard from again. Not Hoffa — that was somebody else's message — but my grandfather had no compunctions against taking decisive action.

And then there's the prostitution, guns, gambling, drugs, human trafficking, protection racket, and more. These ran on a somewhat different financial agreement, since they weren't always a continuing business operation. For one-time deals, The Financier would take a larger cut of the profits, collecting the principal and interest at the same time, but he made certain to keep things going by reinvesting a large part of the cash in follow-up operations.

Need money to dig under a bank, and a special drill to gain access to the vault? Call The Financier. Need to put together a team to rip off a casino and the money to make them look the part? Call The Financier.

Need seed money to make a product on spec and to pay for the commercials to sell it on late-night television? Call The Financier.

That's my grandfather. Believe it or not, he's seen by most people as a good guy. There are parks named after him, and boulevards, hospital wings and university buildings. His funding has propped up research that has saved more lives than he's ruined. Politicians in both major political parties are in office because of his backing and many Ph.D.s have his college grants to thank for their educations.

I remember a time, back when I was still rather young, that I first witnessed how my grandfather operated.

I spent a lot of time living at my grandfather's house, a large mansion he'd "inherited" that included a sizable library. By "sizable," I mean three stories tall, with a cupola on top to let in sunlight. Built-in shelves covered the walls from floor to the base of the cupola, with ladders on each floor to reach the highest levels, and a circular staircase providing access between floors.

A large part of my time was spent in that library, curled up in a comfortable nook built into the shelving on the second floor, my nose buried in a book.

That was where I was when I first understood what my grandfather was doing.

I was, as usual, curled up with a book when my grandfather entered the library, followed by two men. They didn't notice me in the floor above, and I remained still and silent so they wouldn't. I was curious, so I stayed and eavesdropped.

Grandfather sat at his desk near the base of the circular staircase. The two men remained standing on the other side, facing him. One held a hat in his hands, twisting it nervously. The other gestured with his hands as he spoke.

"Financier," he said, "my partner and I want to develop a form of software that will revolutionize the way computers operate, making them simple enough to use that they are no longer limited to major companies and state agencies, but can be used by the average person in his own home."

My grandfather was tall and slender, prematurely gray, and well-educated. He read the Wall Street Journal every day it published, as well as The New York Times and several other newspapers.

"So, you are talking about microcomputers," he said. "You have competition."

"Yes, Financier, a couple of guys in Albuquerque are working on software that would do something similar, and another couple of guys in Menlo Park are working on a new type of microcomputer. We just feel this would be a good time to get into this field."

"I see. And what do you want from me?"

The two looked at each other, then back at my grandfather.

"We think we could do it with $100,000," the one using his hands said.

"How much have you raised so far?"

"$900,000."

"So this would give you a million dollars. What assurance do I have that my investment will produce returns?"

The man sputtered, and tried to spin some mumbo-jumbo about hiring the best people to do the work, and how they couldn't fail because they'd be hiring only people who were proven to know what they were doing.

Grandfather waved his hand, dismissing the argument. "No, here is what you are going to do. Both of you will take out life insurance policies — term or whole life, I don't care, that's up to you. The policies are to be for at least $100,000 each, naming me as beneficiary. You can set larger sums, if you desire, and name other beneficiaries, just so long as I am guaranteed $100,000 in the case of your deaths, each of you."

The man with the gesturing hands gulped, loudly, and the man with the hat dropped it, then hesitated before he finally bent over and picked it up.

"That, of course, is if you don't succeed," my grandfather said. "If you do succeed, then you can switch beneficiaries or allow the policies to lapse, I don't care. In that case, however, because I would be contributing 10 percent of your start-up funding, I would expect to get 10 percent of your gross profits, in perpetuity."

"Until the loan is paid off?" the man with the hands asked.

"Do you not know what 'in perpetuity' means?" my grandfather growled, showing emotion for the first time. "It means 'forever.'"

The two men looked at each other again, hesitating.

My grandfather shrugged. "Or you can leave right now without a penny from me, no harm, no foul. This conversation will not have taken place, and you can get your funding from somewhere else. I wish you the very best of luck."

The man with the hat stammered a moment, then said, "Could — could we think about it and get back to you?"

Grandfather laughed and leaned back. "Of course! I'm not twisting your arm to take this offer. It doesn't expire the minute you walk out the door. You can come back any time, or never. I leave it entirely up to you. But my conditions for investing $100,000 will not change."

The two left rather quickly, and my grandfather looked up at where I thought I was hiding and said, "Do you think they'll be back?"

So he had noticed me!

I thought for a moment, then nodded, got up and descended the staircase to stand in front of his desk, where the others had stood moments earlier. "They've already raised 90 percent. They'll be willing to gamble that they can succeed at this, and will make enough money that 10 percent off the top will seem meaningless."

"How much of a gamble do you think it is?"

"They don't know computers or software, Grandfather. They aren't fully invested in the idea themselves, but think they can get rich off the work of others. That might work for some — you, for example — but it won't for them."

He nodded, and let me go back to reading my book, upstairs.

The two men were back two days later, and walked out with $100,000. Two years later, there was a tragic, fiery traffic accident with two fatalities, and my grandfather received insurance checks totaling $200,000. Their families were well-taken care of, as well.

The home computer industry took off without their help.

CHAPTER 34: FINDING FRED

My grandfather had three sons. My father was the youngest.

The eldest son became a lawyer and went into politics. He has been a senator, a diplomat and a lobbyist. He also has been a conduit for some of my grandfather's financial transactions, both above and below the table.

The second son went into the priesthood. For a time he advised my grandfather on charitable contributions and donations that would benefit the community, then he got caught up in the pedophile scandals and fled both the country and the priesthood. Now he runs an underage brothel in Thailand featuring innocents trafficked in from around the world. You can guess where the financing came from.

Then there's my father. He decided to put the family familiarity with the underworld to good use and became a police officer. He responded to incidents of domestic violence, investigated traffic accidents, chased purse snatchers, taught drug resistance to schoolchildren, rousted panhandlers and shut down drug operations as fast as they popped up, winning accolades and a reputation as a straight-shooter within the law enforcement community.

He also ran a drug operation on the side, shut down the competition through his arrests, used his school connections to get students hooked, allowed drunken drivers to leave accident scenes for a payment that varied by who they were, and forced panhandlers into private fights for the amusement of his cronies.

I had a brother and a sister and several cousins, all steeped in the family business. Yes, even the priest had children; he was no angel.

We all found our particular niches.

I found that I was good at covering things up. You might say I was a cleaner. I didn't kill anyone, but I cleaned up after family members who did.

Some of it was just as simple as sanitizing a crime scene before the police arrived, so that there was no indication that anything unlawful had taken place there. Or if that absence of evidence were considered impossible, then it would be up to me to make certain no sign of family involvement remained, or perhaps to point the focus of the investigation in a totally different direction.

Sleight of hand, misdirection, fabrication of evidence, whatever was needed, I could provide. It turned out I was really good at lying.

It wasn't always family, either. I cleaned for people who had connections with my family.

Say, for example, a school bus is speeding out of control, goes off the road and wraps itself around a tree, killing a third of the students inside and maiming a dozen more for life. It might be that I am called upon to quietly deliver evidence of the driver's psychotic breakdown to the DA. Or perhaps I am able to provide details that show faulty maintenance on the bus' brakes and hydraulic system to lawyers representing bereaved parents, indicating that a member of the school board is directly behind the so-called accident, thus allowing a friend of the family to run for the suddenly empty seat on the board.

I was good at what I did and, frankly, I was proud of it. But it wasn't personal; it was just business. The family business. Some might have considered me a sociopath — heck, it's a label I would have accepted without a qualm.

Bodies disappeared. Evidence collected by police and maintained in constant police custody still managed to be altered between the DA's office and the courthouse. I was directly or indirectly responsible for ... but that would sound like bragging.

While one can take pride in one's work, there can come a point where that pride wears thin. So thin, in fact, that it breaks. Shatters. Completely. And shame replaces it.

What was my breaking point? Well, I can tell you it wasn't my marriage.

Oh yes, I was married for a time. It failed in part because of what I was doing and in part because, well, she got religion in a bad way. I mean, a really bad way. And, well, she ended up going to Thailand and helping run my uncle's brothel.

It hit me hard. I was lonely and depressed, and it showed. I started making mistakes and my grandfather called me to face him at his desk in the library.

"Carter," he didn't say, because he used my real name, not the one the U.S. Marshals Service set me up with, "it has come to my attention that you aren't paying full attention to your job." That, he did say, or at least words to that effect. His tone may have been harsher; I'm not sure. I think I may have been drunk at that point.

The woman I'd promised to honor and cherish and stay with for the rest of my life had run off with my pedophile priest uncle to help run a brothel full of underage prostitutes in Thailand, for God's sake! How was I supposed to react?

"Your problem," my grandfather told me, "is that you don't have enough responsibility."

I thought he was going to punish me. Instead, he rewarded me, in a manner of speaking.

"You should get a dog. I know just the breeder you should see."

"A dog?" I asked. "Responsibility?"

He chuckled. "Of course! You have to take care of a dog. You have to feed it and care for it and take it for walks. You have to come home to let your dog outside when he needs to go outside, or else you have to clean up the mess if he's unable to wait. If you know you won't be home in time, you have to make arrangements for someone else to take care of your dog while you are away. You have to watch for illness, for injury, and take the dog to the vet periodically so he can have his shots and have regular checkups to make certain he has a long and happy life with you."

He gave me the name of a breeder. His breeder. One whose work he was financing, not because he expected a financial return — it wasn't a puppy mill, for God's sake, he loathed those — but because he was wanting a breed of more intelligent dogs that could assist with the family business in ways that family members could not.

His idea was for dogs to be able to act independently of orders. Like border collies, except they wouldn't be working with sheep.

The breeder, on the other hand, had somewhat different ideas that just dovetailed enough with my grandfather's idea that she won the funding. Her plan was, through breeding, to develop a breakthrough in human-animal communications. She wanted a dog that could talk with its owner.

She bred intelligent dogs with dogs that tended to vocalize more than others. I don't mean barking or growling or whimpering, but making sounds as if they were actually attempting to speak.

She tested and experimented and worked on each generation, selecting mates, developing training programs and figuring out other ways to enhance their communications specialties. Surgery was strictly forbidden; all improvement had to come genetically, so it could be passed on from one generation to the next.

My grandfather got the results he wanted. The smartest generation ended up probably smarter than a first-grader. They displayed a better understanding of human vocabulary than a majority of other dogs, but by and large did not gain the ability to speak. Some successful graduates of her breeding program have been used by the military overseas, sniffing out bombs, tracking terrorists and, more often than not, saving lives. Others have gone into law enforcement, doing much the same thing.

As I've said, my grandfather is considered by many to be a "good guy."

So after my grandfather had his little talk with me, I sobered up and made an appointment to meet with the breeder. She had a female that was about due to have puppies, and because of my connection with my grandfather, I could have the pick of the litter.

Normally, for an outsider to acquire one of her dogs, it would have cost $30,000, minimum.

I remember the first day I saw Fred. He had been born the day before and his eyes weren't open yet. He was the runt of the litter, and he squeaked with outrage when his siblings found their mamma's nipple and he couldn't. We didn't know his sex yet; it was way too early. But we called him a "him" then anyway, until we could know for certain.

"The little one's feisty," I told the breeder.

She nodded. "Pity he probably isn't going to survive," she said.

"What do you mean?"

"You see how the others are crowding him out? If he can't figure out how to get in there, and soon, he'll die."

The breeder didn't believe in coddling her dogs. She wanted the best and smartest and strongest, and any puppy that failed to meet her standards was culled from the breeding program.

Something about the littlest puppy spoke to me, and I asked permission to stay and watch. She made me promise not to interfere. Nature had to take its course.

I agreed, although I must confess I thought if he couldn't find his mama's nipple, I'd be willing to hand feed him myself. I just didn't tell the breeder that, because it likely would have gotten me kicked out. She was serious about her program.

I watched him the rest of the day and into the night. I fell asleep outside the pen and awakened the next day to resume vigil.

I had noticed the mother had a particular way of lying down when it came time to feed the puppies, and although there was no way he could see anything yet, the little guy figured out that if he could move from one end of the pack to the middle or, better yet, the other end, he would have a better chance at getting fed first rather than last.

Although he solved the feeding problem, Fred remained the runt. The breeder said he probably wouldn't be bred into the program because of his size. My grandfather wanted larger dogs, intimidating dogs, and he was paying the bills. Fred came from large dogs, but apparently recessive genes kicked in for him instead of dominant genes, and he just did not get large enough.

Which was fine with me. I volunteered to take him, as soon as he was ready, and the breeder was agreeable. Turns out he might not have brought $30,000 after all, since he was a failure for the program, so it was no great loss for her to let me have him free of charge.

No one knew it at the time, not even me, but Fred was a million-dollar dog.

CHAPTER 35: MILLION-DOLLAR DOG

Fred continued to exhibit his intelligence after his eyes opened. He was the first to figure out how to escape the pen. The breeder installed counter measures, and he escaped anyway. Just like at the cat habitat at the zoo, Fred figured out how to take advantage of unrecognized opportunity.

Why was he escaping?

It's because I had pretty much set up residence there.

Apparently I was lonelier than I'd realized, and Fred filled the emptiness. The breeder, thinking of my grandfather's continuing largess, let me stay as much as I wanted, so long as I didn't get in the way or otherwise interfere with her program. Because Fred wasn't going to be part of the program, I was free to work with him however I wished.

So he would escape and find me, no matter where I might be hiding. And I hid in some pretty good hiding places. He always found me.

Always.

I sat down with him and read to him, using children's books to begin with. He studied the pictures in the books, recognizing the relationship between the images and the words I was saying. I helped him, of course, in recognizing the patterns and relationships, then the connections between the stories in the books and what he encountered in real life.

He vocalized a lot, and at some point, it dawned on both the breeder and me that he was attempting to repeat what I was saying. He was trying to talk.

I can only imagine it was like teaching a child with developmental disabilities and a speech impediment, but who was eager to learn and willing to fight his limitations to do the very best he could.

That's the way it seemed to me, anyway.

I know what you're thinking. You've seen in the funniest videos shows on TV, or in YouTube videos, where dogs appear to speak, so maybe it doesn't seem that impossible to you, right?

Well, it's been argued that dogs that seem to talk are just imitating the sounds their owners want them to make, and doing it for the reward of a treat or praise, or the attention. But not that the dogs actually know what they are saying.

You could have a conversation with a dog if it was, in a way, pre-scripted. Train the dog to make the sounds in response to certain stimuli, and it will seem to answer questions.

But that isn't talking. Not really. Or so the argument goes.

But isn't that the way we train our own babies to speak? We get them to imitate the words, you know, like "mama" and "dada," and train them to make these sounds in response to certain stimuli. We reward them for getting it right, and we correct them when they get it wrong.

The only difference I could see in the technique, at least at the rudimentary level, is that the baby has lips and tongue and palate and eventually the muscle control built for speech, while the dog's lips, tongue and palate are different, and the same muscle control just isn't there.

But a truly intelligent dog, with a lot of practice and help and gentle correction and lots of praise, may be able to overcome the limitations of its biological architecture. And learn to form sentences, and understand context, and think for himself without having to be trained with a treat after each minute achievement.

Admittedly, Fred is a freak. None of his siblings developed the ability to speak the way he did. As far as I know, none of their offspring, or those who came later, also learned to speak.

Just Fred.

The breeder decided she wanted Fred to breed anyway, to sire other puppies that might be able to learn to talk. It didn't work out. Fred was shooting blanks. Like a mule, he is sterile.

She never told my grandfather or anyone else about Fred's ability. No one would have believed her anyway, and Fred learned the hazards of speaking out of turn. He has to trust someone before he'll reveal his secret, and his confidants are few.

I took Fred home and continued to work with him, reading more complicated books to him, explaining what they meant, helping him to understand the human-centered world into which he was born.

He wasn't happy with his lot as "just a pet," instead of as an equal, but he seems to have adapted to it. When we are alone, we are equals, Fred and me. When we are in public, we are dog and human, companions, with the two-legged one in charge. Usually.

This didn't happen overnight, of course. It was a long, slow process.

Then there was a time when I came home from one of my cleaning jobs and Fred asked me what I did when I was away.

It wasn't easy to explain to him. My father had hit a drug house, killing the pusher and taking his stashes of drugs and cash. My job was to go in and make the body disappear, clean up the evidence of violence and make it look like the pusher had fled the area, taking everything valuable with him. We wanted the dead man's suppliers to think he'd turned on them and fled.

Fred didn't understand.

There were so many aspects of the situation that were foreign to his point of view. What are drugs and why do people take them? If they need to escape from the way they live, why don't they just change the way they live? They could adopt a dog and love it and take it for walks and spend time together and everything would be wonderful.

Punishment he understood, as sometimes consequences for breaking the rules needs to be demonstrated. A growl and bared teeth, for example, when a sibling gets too close to a treat that is clearly yours.

But to kill something, and not consuming it as food, perplexed him. Then to realize I had made the food go away, without eating it myself or making it available to others, just didn't seem right to him. I tried to explain that we humans don't eat each other — not usually anyway — after one kills another. We had to agree that this was a puzzle that would have to be explored later, after he'd had more experience and a greater understanding of humanity's peculiarities.

The rest of it just became more and more bewildering for Fred. Why would I want to take what is real and true, and attempt to change it to something that is not?

People think you need religion to provide a moral compass, and for a lot of people that's true. I met the pastor of a church once who claimed that, without his religion, he might be a rapist or a murderer. All I could do was thank God that this genuine sociopath had his religion to keep him in check.

But dogs don't need a religion to be moral. They see things in a simpler way. The food dish is empty, or it has food in it. A squirrel is in the yard, or it isn't. When you tease them, like performing a magic trick, and what they expect to see doesn't happen, they get frustrated or offended. You have violated their moral values.

What I was doing was violating Fred's moral values. It made him uncomfortable, and that eventually made me uncomfortable, too.

Fred continued to ask me questions each time I came home from a cleaning job. Simple, innocent questions that only a dog or a child could ask, and the answers grew harder and harder to justify.

I began to experience empathy for the people who were being hurt by the actions of my family. I let it affect my attitude as I approached my job.

That's a bad thing to do in a family like mine.

CHAPTER 36: THE FINAL STRAW

As Fred was educating me about a way of life that ran counter to my family upbringing, he also opened my world again as a human being. After my wife left me, I had avoided forming a relationship with anyone new except, of course, Fred and the breeder whose program produced him.

But Fred was friendly and outgoing and smart, and he seemed to recognize that, in addition to himself, I needed human companionship.

Our neighbor was young, attractive and single, and she also had a dog. It was only natural that Fred would smooth the way to our chatting, then walking our dogs together, then spending more time together until we became intimate.

I've already referred to her as River, although that wasn't her real name. (When you're in the program, everything changes.) We spent a lot of time together. We talked, a lot, about ourselves and, of course, our dogs. Fred was learning about speaking to humans and at this point was keeping his ability to himself. We'd watched some movies where talking animals were exploited and Fred drew lessons from this.

I blame myself for what ultimately happened. It wasn't with Fred; it was with River.

I let slip one of my "special projects," thinking I'd wow her with my creativity. I won't get into specifics. Let's just say the evidence collected by the police wasn't what was presented in court, even though it never left the required chain of custody, and a friend of the family was released on a technicality.

Sure, Fred had me feeling guilty about a lot of what I was doing, but that didn't mean I couldn't take pride in my work, right?

Yeah, well, I regret everything today.

River turned in a tip about the incident. She thought she'd been clever and had protected me from being found out.

It didn't matter how anonymous she kept it. Word got to the person who knew all about it anyway, and he figured out pretty quickly how the word got out.

Fred and River's dog were in another room, napping after having spent a long day playing at the dog park, and River and I were curled up together on a couch, watching TV, when I heard a knock at the side door.

I excused myself from River, went through the kitchen and answered the door. It was my father, the police officer. Lieutenant Dad, I called him, at times. When they were good times. Other times, he was Sir.

When I opened the door, he was frowning.

"You alone?" he asked, entering without invitation.

"No, Sir," I said. "I have company."

"Your neighbor?"

"Yes ..."

"I need to have a word with her," he said.

He followed the sound of the TV into the living room, where River had gotten up from the couch and was looking in our direction.

She said my name, with an uplift in her voice that made it a question.

My father said nothing, but pulled out his pistol and shot her in the face.

I screamed as she fell to the floor without a sound, and he fired a second time, making certain the bullet went through her brain.

Then he turned to me, the gun pointed at my chest.

I froze in place. My ears were ringing from the sound of the two discharges in the confined space of the living room. I couldn't hear the TV. If the dogs were alert and barking, I couldn't hear them either.

My father's mouth was moving. I couldn't hear what he was saying and shortly it became clear to him why I wasn't responding to his orders. He gestured for me to roll River's body up in the floor rug on which she had fallen, and as I did so he stepped into an adjoining room and fired the pistol twice more.

I knew without looking that he was shooting at the dogs. There wasn't anything I could do. I felt stunned, trapped in an emotional web of terror, loss and anger, and all I could do was whatever he told me to do.

As my hearing slowly came back, he told me to pick up River's body and to follow him. We went out the side door, where I saw that he had left a shovel. He picked it up, gave me a "follow me" gesture, then flicked on a flashlight and led the way down my back yard.

My house was one that bordered a wooded area left natural by the developers. A creek ran through it, and the esthetics of having nature so nearby outweighed the cost of cutting down the trees and installing a culvert to trap the flowing waters. Homeowners occasionally complained about skunks and beavers that came calling from time to time, but for the most part having a wooded area nearby was a welcome escape from city living.

I felt differently about it, though, that night when I followed my father into the trees, carrying my dead girlfriend's body over my shoulder, weeping, wondering if Fred was dead, too, and if I was going to be next.

"Quit sniveling," my father said. He dropped the shovel at my feet. "Put her down and start digging."

He stepped back far enough that I couldn't use the shovel as a weapon against him. He let me see in the gleam from the flashlight that the pistol was out again and pointed at me.

I dug. And dug. I had to cut through roots with the edge of the shovel, and kept digging. My hands grew raw, blistered, and the blisters popped. My muscles ached, and my back was punishing my unusual activity with sharp pains when my father told me to stop and get out of the hole.

At his order, I rolled River, still wrapped in the rug, into the shallow grave.

My father stood there, shining the flashlight in my eyes.

"I ought to do you, too," he said.

We stood there, silent for a moment, then he said, "You talked to her, boy. You told her something you shouldn't have. Word got out and I've had the devil's own time putting a stop to things before they got out of hand. The Financier and I discussed this, and we agreed that you needed to be taught a lesson. I wanted to do more, but he said this should be enough."

I said nothing. He was still pointing the pistol at me. My father rarely went against my grandfather's orders, and I didn't want this to be one of those rare occasions.

"Cover her up and go home," he said. "Make her go away, as you do so well when you aren't thinking with your dick. And keep your damn mouth shut in the future!"

He left me there, in the darkness, taking the flashlight with him.

I stood there for a long time, listening to him leave, then listening to the silence he left behind him. My eyes gradually adjusted to the dark, aided by a gibbous moon glowing through the trees, and I slowly shoveled the soil back into the hole, my back protesting with every move, the shovel handle becoming slick with what I was sure was sweat and blood.

As I tamped down the soil and tried to make it look like a grave had not just been covered up there, I heard a rustling in the woods nearby. It didn't sound big as if my father'd had a change of heart and was returning to finish me off. It sounded small, like a dog.

I dropped the shovel and Fred leaped into my arms, licking my face and cleaning the tears off my cheeks.

I hugged him until he protested and I let him down. My father may have shot at him, but he'd missed. He hadn't missed with River's dog, and I later buried it next to River.

With this, my conversion was complete. Fred had given me a newfound sense of moral purpose — a guilty conscience, if you like — and this cemented everything in place. I could not continue to live this way.

Mindful of my family's connections, I couldn't go to just anyone. District attorneys, judges, police unions, so many people were involved in one way or another with the family business, I'd be signing my own death warrant if I spoke to the wrong person first. The way River had.

I couldn't even go to anyone in our congressional delegation, or the governor's office, or the state attorney general.

I ended up going federal, and contacted the U.S. Marshals Service. Even then, I didn't go through normal channels. I had to find someone I could work with, who would be willing to work with me, and who wouldn't turn me in and get me killed.

Fred, again, helped me. He's an excellent judge of character. He tells me it comes with his sense of smell. He knows when someone just doesn't smell right, and when someone is trustworthy.

I found a trustworthy U.S. Marshal and turned myself in. I showed her where the body was buried and I was arrested, but was kept out of the system where my father could reach me. I made a deal with the federal prosecutor, testified before a federal grand jury, and went into hiding.

That's my story, pretty much, as I told it to Julie. Most of it is true. I may have embellished some.

But Fred will vouch for me.

CHAPTER 37: WHY THIS HOUSE?

"Well, Fred? Is that what happened?"

"Yeh!"

I slipped him a treat. He got up on his hind legs and did a little dance, then ate the treat.

"Funny!" she said.

"One thing I left out," I said. "You need to know about it, so you'll know how serious this is."

"It gets more serious than two bullets in the head?"

I nodded.

"Right after I agreed to testify, the U.S. Marshals sent some people to my house to get things I'd need when disappearing forever. Just a few items I didn't want to leave behind. I'd be changing my style of clothing, so my wardrobe was out. But Fred had some favorite toys, and I had some CDs and a few other things I wanted to keep.

"About three minutes after the agents entered my house, it exploded, leaving no survivors."

"Oh my God," she said.

"I insisted on being driven by before leaving town. There was a smoking crater where my house once stood. Houses on both sides as well as across the street also were damaged. The news on TV that night blamed a gas leak, but I knew better. It was a bomb intended for me.

"So you can't breathe a word of this to anyone. Not your best friend, not your parents, not even your priest in confession. Heck, don't even whisper it to the lions at the zoo. You never know who might be listening. And this is for your safety as well as Fred's and mine.

"My family doesn't care who they hurt."

Julie got up and went to the window to look out. Then, apparently thinking about my story, she closed the curtains and stepped away from the windows.

"How do you live, knowing they want you dead?" she asked.

I shrugged, then gestured to Fred, who jumped up onto my lap for a brief cuddle and head scratch.

"I have Fred and he has me. We watch out for each other, and we lie low." I paused to think about what I'd just said, then snorted. "OK, we try to lie low. It isn't easy when one day you discover you have a foul-smelling, blood-sucking monster living under your floor."

"Why your floor?" she asked.

"What do you mean?"

"What is so special about this house that a thing like that would be living under it when you moved in? I mean, this is a big city, with a lot of empty buildings. Heck, when Walmart gets tired of dealing with leaks in their roof, they build a new store and abandon the old one. And if it isn't Walmart, then it's some other bankrupt manufacturer or business or foreclosed homeowner who moves out, leaving an empty nest practically designed to meet the needs of this thing.

"Why here? Why this house?"

I told her what Penny had told me about the house, how it had been acquired by one federal agency and put into use by a different federal agency for Fred and me to live in.

"So this was a meth lab," she said.

"That's what I'm told."

"That still doesn't explain the thing under the floor. There are meth houses all over the city. You practically can't throw a crack pipe without hitting one in some neighborhoods. *Why this house?*"

Fred and I looked at each other. When it was clear neither one of us had an answer, he jumped down and went into the kitchen for a drink of water. I shook my head at Julie.

"No idea."

"Who had this house before the meth chefs?"

I shrugged. "She didn't say; I didn't ask."

"Do you have a computer? Internet access? Oh, never mind, I have a smart phone." She pulled the phone from where she kept it inside her bra and started tapping.

"What are you doing?"

She came over and sat next to me, leaning into me. I put my arm around her, pulled her closer, and watched as her fingers practically blurred against the glowing screen.

She called up the county assessor's website. "What's your address again?"

I told her, and she entered it into a search field.

A moment later, she had a list of the previous owners of this property and the dates of ownership change. "OK, this is who owns the house now, and this is who owned the house previously. I'd guess that would be the meth people. Before them it says, um, Nathanial Rysart.

"So now let's look up Nathanial Rysart," she said. "Look, an obituary."

"I guess we won't be calling him up and asking any questions, huh?"

"Shh! Listen to this: 'In his 80s, Dr. Rysart became interested in synthetic biology, which is a form of genetic engineering. He told colleagues he was nearing a breakthrough in developing a biological alternative to dialysis, but he died before he could publish any results.'"

"'Synthetic biology'?"

She typed into a search engine, paused a moment, then said, "Here's a story on 'Do-It-Yourself Genetic Engineering' in *The New York Times Magazine* from a few years ago. Hang on ..."

She read into the story as I leaned my head back and closed my eyes.

"OK, synthetic biologists are involved in mixing and matching genetic codes, taking a little bit from one creature and a little bit from another, and putting them together into something that has never been seen before on this planet," she said.

"Frankenstein," I said.

"Not exactly. It says here one company developed a bacterium that can secrete a biofuel similar to diesel. Another company converted a yeast to fight malaria. Get this: There are things called BioBricks, which are kind of like DNA-based Legos. Thousands of them in an open-source genetic library, each one catalogued to do something different.

"It doesn't even require someone who knows what she's doing. The story says these things can be put together like a kid building a 'fortress on a living-room carpet.' And this story came out in 2010 — imagine the advances they've made since then!"

I got up and started pacing. "So we have a scientist, this Dr. Rysart, who was working on developing something that could replace a dialysis machine. It would need to siphon blood from a patient, filter the poisons out the way the kidneys do, then it would return the blood all shiny and new.

"In an ideal world, this would have worked and he would have won the Nobel Prize in Medicine for it," I said.

"But this isn't an ideal world."

"It sounds like he was trying this on his own, here at home, perhaps, instead of in an established laboratory, with all of the safeguards that would require. Rysart was in his 80s, which suggests he may have been retired. So, a little bit of this from a tick, and a little bit of that from a leech, and perhaps a pinch of something from some creature that shuns the light, and instead of a living dialysis machine he accidentally creates our monster."

She gestured for me to sit next to her again, so I did. She was nice to sit next to.

"Say the creature was started in a home laboratory," she said. "The obit didn't say how Dr. Rysart died."

"I'm guessing 'cardiac arrest,'" I said. "Hearts do tend to stop beating when there is no blood left to pump."

"Wouldn't the police have drawn a connection between his death and that of the family down the street?"

"Not to mention the people running the meth lab," I said. "Official reports are that they died of meth overdose, but I hear unofficially they, too, were victims of this thing.

"It's possible the police have made connections, and we don't know this because we aren't involved in their investigation — which is just fine by me. But if different personnel are involved in each investigation, and the official records carry the official line — cardiac arrest, meth overdose, carbon monoxide poisoning, fire-related deaths, hantavirus infection — then the police won't see the common thread."

"Surely the coroner's office would pick up on that."

"Oh, good point! I forgot about them. OK, so we can assume the police are aware of the connections. But that doesn't mean they know about the creature, or its origins. They may think some human group is behind this: terrorists, or a cult, satanic or otherwise. But that doesn't matter. I can't consult with them or it would set me up with my family."

"It's up to us, isn't it?"

"Looks that way."

"Well, crap."

"Look on the bright side."

"What's that?"

"We have an advantage. We have Fred."

CHAPTER 38: DISCOVERED

We spent the night in each other's arms. Again. I told myself I could get used to this. Fred seemed agreeable with the idea as well. As for Julie, well, she left no doubt in my mind.

"But first we need to take care of this thing," she said.

"Agreed."

"So what's your plan?"

I laughed. "You know, if this were a movie, the plot would be fairly predictable. We'd have a plan, all right, but the moment we implemented it and met up with the creature, the plan would fall apart. One or both of us then would end up being menaced by the creature and, just as things are looking their bleakest, we come up with a daring and surprisingly effective solution, killing the monster and saving the day."

"That sort of thing happens in novels, too," she pointed out.

My one and only concern was to kill off the creature and any of its spawn, protect the lives of those who are dear to me, and survive to fight another day. OK, that's three concerns, but still.

In any case, nothing happened the way I jokingly predicted.

Julie left for work, after we'd both promised we'd think about this during the day, then Fred and I took an early morning walk. I've found that long walks are an excellent way to clear the mind — assuming, that is, that Fred hasn't detected the trail of a blood-sucking monster.

We had lunch at the sidewalk café, and I noticed someone trying to pretend not to look at me. But he was looking at me anyway, then looking at his smart phone and back at me. Not good!

"Fred, we've got to go," I said, standing and taking up his leash.

It looked like the man was about to point the camera of his phone at us. I turned away with Fred and said, "Gotta hustle."

Taking the long way home, wanting to make sure the only tail we had was attached to Fred, along the way I called our favorite U.S. Marshal.

"Penny," I said. I was having trouble catching my breath, like I'd climbed 20 flights of stairs. Panic will do that to a person. "I think we've been made."

"What happened?"

I described the man at the café and his interest in something on the smart phone that, judging from his actions, appeared to have something to do with me.

"Just a minute," Penny said, and I was on hold for at least three city blocks and a quick trip through a dollar store's loading dock and out a bar's back door as well. If anyone was following us, they were getting a workout. I know I was. Fred seemed to be doing just fine.

"You still there, Carter?"

"So far," I said.

"It looks like someone has posted a reward for you on the Dark Web. There are photos of you as you were, and artist's renderings of what you might look like if you grew a beard, shaved your head, tinted your hair or made other changes in your appearance."

"Great," I said.

"It gets better," she said. "The reward is $25 million."

"Twenty-five! I'm almost tempted to turn myself in for that!"

"Except you wouldn't live to enjoy it," she said.

"There is that," I said. "What am I going to do?"

"Well, first, never go back to that café," she said. "We'll monitor the Dark Web and see if there is any further movement there. And you, well, lie lower still. Stay home, have minimal contact with anyone. Take a different route any time you go somewhere, if you must go somewhere. Make note of any strange vehicles or people in your neighborhood, and keep your doors and windows locked."

"I do that already," I said. "Mostly."

"Then do it even more," she said. "Keep Fred with you at all times. They might try to take him to draw you out.

"Meanwhile, we'll try to speed things up on this end. The sooner we can get your family behind bars, the better things will be. I'll have a word with the U.S. Attorney."

It sounded like she was wrapping up the phone call. "Before you go, Marshal, I've got something I need to tell you. I've met a woman ..."

"No!" she interrupted. "Don't have anything to do with her. Don't see her, don't call her, just drop her. If she doesn't put you in danger, you'll put her in danger. It's a no-win for everyone."

I was silent as I tried to think of something to say. She beat me to it.

"Oh, Carter, it's already too late, isn't it?"

"Um, yeah. It is. I've, ah, told her everything."

"Well, crap! That just — wait! I know you, Carter. You ran everything by Fred before you did all this, didn't you?"

"Yes. And Fred was OK with her."

She took a deep breath. "All right then. Give me her name and particulars so I can run a check on her to see if the Justice Department feels the same way about her as Fred does."

I told her what I knew about Julie, then I said, "There's one thing more."

"Of course there is, Carter. What is it?"

"We tracked down the creature and, I think, killed it, after it had fed on a group of homeless people."

"Was that the hantavirus story?"

"That's the one."

"Law enforcement there is getting pretty creative about its cover-ups," she said. "I had no inkling."

"But Fred says there are more out there. I don't know if it's adults like this thing we killed, or younger offspring, but the battle isn't over yet."

I dodged into a convenience store and pretended to stand in line for an ATM, watching out the window for anyone who might still be following us.

"You need to let the local authorities handle this, Carter."

"You're right, of course, except for one thing. They don't know what I know — and you know I can't tell them."

She sighed. "I know."

"So the question is: Do I keep after this thing, or do I lie low and watch the locals ruin any chance of putting a stop to it? Look, Marshal, I know you can't step in and tell them what's going on, because they wouldn't have any reason to believe you. No local cop wants to believe the government agent who 'knows what's going on,' especially not when the local cop has already made up his mind. And coming from me, with the reputation I'm about to get in federal court for spinning lies, it's a no-win situation."

I couldn't actually hear it over the phone, but I knew she was shaking her head. "You're a grown man, Carter. And I suspect that dog of yours has more sense than you and me rolled together. Just know that any mistake you make is your own, come what may."

I was back on the street again, feeling like the way was clear, finally. "I've always owned my mistakes, Marshal. Growing up in my family, my mistakes were the only things I truly could claim ... as uniquely mine."

"You're allowed your mistakes, Carter. I just don't want to see you make a fatal one; I like you too much for that."

"And here I thought you didn't care," I said.

"You're like an unexplained rash, you know? You tend to grow on a person."

I laughed. "Let me know when you've cleared Julie of impure thoughts and deeds; I want to be the one who inspires those."

"Too much information, Carter!"

Fred and I made it home without further incident. I kept watch on the street through a crack in the curtains until Julie pulled up; Fred acted as if everything was normal.

Whatever *normal* is.

CHAPTER 39: RECORDS

I told Julie about the man at the café, and what Penny Ransome told me about the $25 million bounty on my head.

"I hope you don't think I'd have anything to do with that!" she said.

"I trust you and, more importantly, Fred trusts you — even if you do hang out with cats all day."

"But the U.S. Marshal doesn't," she guessed.

"She doesn't know you. Of course she doesn't trust you. I hope it doesn't bother you that she's doing a background check on you, and probably has been doing it since the moment we got off the phone."

She glared at me for a moment, then her gaze softened.

"When she finds my juvenile record and opens it ..."

"Those are supposed to stay sealed," I interrupted.

"Of course they are, but she's a fed with a need to know, so she's going to know. When she reads about my misspent youth, she'll see I was a tomboy who got caught burglarizing a vacant house — it was my third, actually, but they never pinned the other two on me — and who got caught shoplifting little knickknacks from the local Woolworth store, and who got caught in possession of less than an ounce of marijuana without an opportunity to smoke any of it.

"Then I came of age and everything I did became a matter of public record — that is, everything that I was caught doing. Marijuana again. I spent six months in jail, after having actually smoked it this time, and haven't touched it since.

"I also spent a few weeks in jail after being pepper-sprayed and arrested during a rally protesting a scheduled speaker at my university. The speaker, who was a former grand dragon of the Ku Klux Klan, canceled the speech. The charges against me were dropped, but they're still a matter of public record.

"Speeding tickets, parking tickets, littering tickets ... let's see, what else? I've thrown away my votes on third-party candidates more often than I care to recall, and have never voted a straight-party ticket. I once sent a fan letter to Fidel Castro; I suspect my parents intercepted it and burned it, because I never received a response. Which is probably a good thing, since I came to despise that old man for what he did to the Cuban people. Well, him and the sanctions ham-fistedly applied by the U.S. without regard for the well-being of the poor in Cuba." She shook her head, as if throwing off that line of thought.

"I've always loved lions and tigers and wanted to become a veterinarian who specializes in wild animals, but the time I lost from my studies those few weeks in jail convinced me that my heart wasn't in it as much as I thought it was, so I changed majors to accounting."

"Accounting!" I said. "But you're ..."

"A big cat researcher at the zoo," she said. "Yes, I just couldn't stay away. I can still do your taxes next spring, if you like.

"Oh, and about that $25 million bounty on your head? You've told me about your family. Do you believe they'd actually pay that amount to find you? I certainly don't. That's way too much. For Osama bin Laden, sure, but not for Earl Carter, or whatever your real name is.

"If I were to turn you in, I'd get nothing from your family, and I'd lose you, too." She paused for a moment, then said, "I kind of like being with you."

She smiled. "Close your mouth, Earl, unless you're about to say something."

I shook my head and closed my mouth. Then, "I think I understand the tattoo now."

Her smile widened to a toothy grin. "Yes?"

She had a small cartoonish tiger tattoo, lighting what appeared to be a doobie with a fiery bill of indeterminate denomination, discretely located in a private place that I will leave up to your imagination.

"Did I tell you I love it?"

"Want to see it again?"

Fred barked from the doorway into the kitchen.

"Absolutely," I said, "but I think Fred is concerned that we're wasting time when we could be hunting for whatever it is we need to be hunting."

"We really need to name that thing," she said.

I got up from the couch, turned and gave her a hand up, and we followed Fred into the kitchen.

"I've been thinking about it," I said. "If ol' Doc Rysart designed it, we could call it Rysart's monster."

"Like Frankenstein's monster."

"Exactly!"

"But most people drop the 'monster' part and call Dr. Frankenstein's creation just 'Frankenstein.' I think it would be disrespectful to Dr. Rysart's inspiration to have people end up calling it a 'Rysart.'"

"Assuming, that is, people ever learn of the Rysart's existence," I said.

"There! You did it yourself! You didn't call it 'Rysart's monster.'"

"That was intentional," I said. "And in my defense, please note that I called it 'the Rysart.'"

"'Rysart' or 'the Rysart,' you still prove my point."

Fred barked again, reminding us why we were now in the kitchen.

On the dining table, I earlier had spread a topographical map of the area, including the zoo and its undeveloped adjacent property. I had found the map online and printed it out in pieces, so now the table was partly covered with 8 1/2-by-11-inch sheets of paper.

We sat down next to each other and looked over the map.

But first ...

"I've got it!" I said. "I've been saying this thing looks a lot like Nosferatu, the Dracula rip-off from the early days of German cinema. We could call it a 'Rysferatu.'"

She smiled and shook her head; she couldn't believe I'd just said that.

"OK, until further notice, Rysferatu it is," I announced.

Fred barked.

"OK, Fred, I hear you," I said. I lifted him onto the table so he could see the map, too. He carefully stayed off the pages, so that they weren't disturbed on the table.

I pointed out a section of the map about a third of the way between the road we'd used to access the property and the zoo grounds, and said, "Best I've been able to figure, this is about where the tent city was."

Julie nodded and traced her finger along the contours to where a waterfall and pool at the base of a bluff were depicted. "And this is where we found the, ah, what was that again?"

"'Rysferatu,'" I said.

"Yeah, where we found the ... 'Rysferatu.'" Somehow she made the word sound sticky, like hot bubble gum you've just stepped in.

"Are there other caves in the area?" I asked, trying to shove aside a sudden image in my head of sticky bubble gum.

"There's one more, a shallow one above the one we found the creature in —"

"The Rysferatu?"

"OK, the one where we found the Rysferatu. I don't think the third cave is deep enough to safely hide something that can't abide the light," she said. "There may be something else inside the cave where we found it."

She paused to see if I was going to interrupt, and when I didn't, she continued. "Egg sacs, maybe. A second Rysferatu, although I have my doubts about that. Could this one still be alive? Despite what we did to it?"

"Still alive! We ruptured that thing's belly and the blood practically exploded all over us!" I protested.

"Yes, and we jumped and ran," she said. "We went home, not once checking to see if the Rysferatu still lived."

"Oh!" I said, sharply. In hindsight, what had seemed like the right thing to do now looked terribly wrong.

"'Oh' indeed," she responded. "We just don't know enough about that thing, and how it responds to light, to know whether we sliced it in half and killed it, or just ripped it open enough that it bled out."

"If it's still alive, we at least must have hurt it," I pointed out. "Perhaps set it back some, since we forced it to lose all of that blood. It probably will need to feed again to do whatever it's going to do."

"The Rysferatu laid at least one egg sac, the one Fred found, after drinking from those poor people in the group home," Julie said, thinking aloud. "After gorging itself on all of those people in the tent city, it was probably going to lay a bunch more egg sacs, and we interrupted that. I hope."

I nodded. "So, if it survived, assuming it's healed from what we did to it, then the Rysferatu is going hunting again. If not tonight, then soon. What do you think? The zoo?"

"No. The zoo might work for its hatchlings, since they would spread out and target individuals. But the Rysferatu has shown a tendency to specialize in human victims." She paused, then said, "Oh God!"

"What?"

"It *could be* the zoo. Most likely, anyway. This weekend is the Lions of the Savannah Scouting Retreat. It's an overnighter where Cub Scouts around fourth or fifth grade come to learn about the big cats and their role in the

African Savannah. They picnic on the grounds, go on a night hike when the zoo is closed to the public, and get a behind-the-scenes look at how the zoo handles its big cats and tries to preserve a Savannah-like setting for them.

"The program eventually pulls them into the Education Center, where they do some hands-on stuff, then they settle down in sleeping bags to spend the rest of the night there. Groups can range in size from 15 to 120, including chaperones."

"Sounds like fun," I said.

"It usually is. And they usually aren't attacked in their sleep."

CHAPTER 40: PREPARATIONS

"This weekend, you say," I said.

"That's what I said," she said.

"Let's go hunting," I said.

Fred barked.

We stopped along the way to get two more tactical flashlights and some other supplies we might need.

The flashlights were even more powerful than the one I'd wielded before, shining a beam at an advertised 2,000 Lumens that the company claimed would carry more than 1,000 feet. The price was reasonable, I thought, and it beat the daylights out of the other flashlight's 600 Lumens. There were other tactical flashlights that were brighter, but considering what the other flashlight had done to the Rysferatu in the cave, I figured the brighter beams would be more than sufficient for the task.

We also equipped ourselves with a heavy duty canvas bag, gloves for both of us, and a large pet carrier. If the Rysferatu was still out there, we were hoping to capture it rather than kill it. Proof in hand is much more effective than wild claims and a drying red smear on the ground.

Fred and I stayed in the car, lying low, while Julie made the purchases. We had to make several stops to find everything we needed.

While she was out at the third store, a surplus supply business, my phone rang. It was the U.S. Marshal.

"She checks out," Penny said.

"I'm not surprised, but it's good to have confirmation."

"Your Julie Evans had a rough start, but she's done well in recent years. Fred comes through again."

"He's good that way."

"You're whispering. So what are you up to now?"

"Fred and I are laying low while, at the same time, we're arming ourselves to hunt the Rysferatu."

"The what?"

"It's what we decided to call this creature. It's a Rysferatu."

"I don't want to know," she said. "Jesus!" she added, then she hung up.

"I don't think she likes what we named the creature," I told Fred.
He just huffed and wagged his tail.

CHAPTER 41: BACK TO THE CAVES

Julie stopped the car near where we'd parked earlier. Police tape stretched across the trail, and we sat for a moment, eyeing the woods. The day was sunny and mild, but the woods seemed ominous and foreboding. A breeze rustled the leaves, making it look like the trees were just waiting to grab us as we ventured near. I felt uneasy, as if someone already had my grave dug and was just waiting for me to fall into it.

"Either it's still in there, or its offspring are, or both," I said.

"You're a master of the obvious, you know that?"

"It's a gift."

We got out, checked our weapons — the lights came on and even in the daylight dazzled the trees, then we switched them off — and with Fred in the lead, we entered the hunting grounds.

The trail through the trees was different from before. It was wider now and showed the passage of countless feet. The investigators, no doubt, and the coroner's crew, and the passage of body bags containing people whose only crime was being homeless and seeking a communal place to spend their nights. Someone had cleared the litter, and it was obvious from breaks in the underbrush that the investigation had not limited itself to the trail, but had spread out through the woods as well.

We came to the branch in the trail, and another segment of police tape stretched across both routes.

"Looks like they were thorough," I said, softly.

"That's good," Julie said. "Do you think they found anything?"

"No idea."

We checked the tent city first. The clearing had been, well, cleared: every tent, every article of clothing, every fast food container and chewing gum wrapper and bottle of whatever had been brought in to drink. It looked like the tent city site had been vacuumed, leaving behind nary a leaf, twig or questionable insect.

"I think they found everything," I said.

Julie nodded, and we backtracked up the trail and headed toward the waterfall.

This route appeared less traveled, but it still showed signs of passage.

"Many men, on foot, with pistols, Kemosabe," I said.

"Shut up," she said.

"Too soon?"

"You've done this too many times. Have a little respect."

"Sorry, Ma'am. Old habits die hard."

She stopped me by tugging on my arm, pulled me close, gave me a kiss that left me breathless, and again said, "Shut up. We're hunting." She moved on like a cat. A big cat.

I nodded, glanced at Fred who was looking back at me, and I maintained radio silence as we doggedly moved on, continuing to parallel the stream toward the waterfall.

We came to the pool at the base of the cliff, and the water pouring through the jaws of the collapsed cave looked pretty much the same as it had the last time we were here. Fred took the lead, essentially running up the steep slope to the first cave.

He did not sneeze. It was clear.

Julie and I followed at a slower pace. Hands and feet just did not match the agility of a smaller body with four legs and strategically placed toenails that, admittedly, needed trimming, but were well-suited for this sort of work.

We reached the first cave and I helped launch Fred toward the second one, just as we had the last time.

Sure enough, he stood at the entrance to the cave and sneezed.

Since the sun was still out, and would be shining on the far entrance to the cave, Julie and I went in with lights on full. We weren't taking any chances this time and flashed the bright beams into every nook and cranny we could find.

We found egg sacs hidden here and there in the cave, inside crevices and tucked in behind stone formations that would have protected them from outside light. The beams cast by the tactical flashlights fried the egg sacs just as surely as a red hot skillet would have fried chicken eggs.

The odor was disgusting but we did not shirk our duty.

We eliminated a dozen or more of them. I lost count after a while. Fred backed us up, making certain we didn't overlook any that he could detect.

We made a good team.

Then Fred went on to the third and last cave, and pronounced it clear.

Later, at the base of the cliff, just out of the spray of the waterfall, Julie said, "I didn't see any sign of the Rysferatu, other than the egg sacs."

"Yeah. Either it escaped or the authorities found it and carted it away. Me, I think it survived and escaped."

I nodded my head toward Fred, who was moving from side to side, his nose to the ground, like a Jack Russell terrier mix doing an impersonation of a bloodhound. "Fred thinks so, too."

He suddenly barked and darted into the underbrush.

"Come Watson, the game is afoot," I said.

Julie groaned. "First Tonto and the Lone Ranger, and now Sherlock Holmes. Next you'll be telling Luke you're his father!"

We plunged into the underbrush behind Fred. It wasn't the same as following a well-trodden footpath through the woods. Lush growth overhead cast the woods in shadow, hiding each obstacle and disguising its nature until we found it out by stumbling into it. We battled creepers and vines, thorny branches and roots that thrust out of the ground to snag at unwary ankles, and very real risks of contact with poison ivy, poison oak and poison sumac. I rehearsed in my mind all the things I'd read and seen about dealing with accidental contact with the less savory plants, then those thoughts fled when we emerged from the underbrush back in the clearing once occupied by the tent city.

Fred darted around the clearing, barked again and plunged into the vegetation on the far side.

I followed and almost immediately got whipped across the face by a branch. Fortunately, it had missed my eye by about a thumb's width, but I could feel blood trickling down my cheek. I wiped at the blood with my hand.

"Fred, wait up," I called, and again we followed him into the undeveloped wilderness.

Now the way was worse than before. Between the waterfall and the camp, the ground had been fairly level. Now it was developing a slant toward the creek that ran through the area. No longer as concerned about poisonous vegetation, I was worried about losing my footing and sliding into something that didn't agree with me, like brambles or a disgruntled honey badger, or a sudden, bone-jarring drop-off.

Then I heard Fred sneeze.

CHAPTER 42: THE RYSFERATU

"Fred, did you find something?"

"Yeh!"

When we came upon him, he was in guard mode, the hair on his back raised and bristly, lips pulled back to display his teeth.

He appeared to be intimidating a very large, old tree that had, at its base, a hollow area that receded upward into the heart of the trunk.

"In there?"

"Yeh!"

Julie and I went to work, digging out the large, heavy, canvas sack that she'd bought along with the tactical flashlights, and we pulled the mouth of the bag snugly around the opening in the trunk, essentially fashioning a trap for the Rysferatu.

Since the interior of the reinforced bag introduced an early darkness to the creature's home in the tree, I hoped it would descend and enter the bag, thus being captured.

It was a simple plan, with dozens of ways it could go wrong, and of course it did.

The Rysferatu simply didn't come out.

Julie and I looked at each other. "What now?" I asked. "Pound on the tree trunk to drive it out?"

She shook her head. "At the zoo, when we have an animal unwilling to cooperate, we're trained that doing that is nonproductive."

"So what is productive?"

"A bribe," she said. "A favorite treat often will do the trick."

"What sort of treat do we have to entice a Rysferatu?"

She produced a tissue and dabbed against my bleeding cheek, pulling back a blood-stained piece of bait.

"Loosen the bag a bit," she said.

I eased it loose across the top, and she dropped the bloody tissue inside, after which I retightened its grip on the tree trunk.

And we waited.

"How hungry is it?" I said, not expecting an answer.

"It may be considering its options," she said. "It knows we're here. If it can smell, it smells the blood, but it also smells the canvas bag, and that unfamiliar odor may be overpowering the scent of the blood. Shh!"

We heard a noise from inside the tree trunk, a skittering sound as if something were descending the hollow space.

I had an uncomfortable realization it was about to taste my blood. I felt a surprise touch to my throat and realized it was my own hand, moving there without conscious volition.

My attention was called back to the tree moments later as the canvas bag dipped and sagged with the weight of a sudden occupant.

"Now!" Julie said, and we clinched the mouth of the bag tight and pulled it away from the tree. The Rysferatu was inside.

It wasn't happy.

It fought and squirmed and struggled against the bag, but the heavy canvas held as if designed for this purpose. It helped that the creature was probably still weakened from the blood-loss it had suffered when we'd hit it with light earlier. I held the bag at arm's length as Julie aimed her flashlight ready to beam the creature down if it managed to break free of the canvas.

Fred checked the hole in the tree to confirm that the Rysferatu was indeed no longer inside, and that it had not left behind any egg sacs, then we made ready to leave. The creature fought against captivity and made holding the canvas bag difficult.

"It's like an angry bobcat in there," Julie said, as we made our way through the woods back toward the car.

Fortunately it wasn't very heavy. I figured its size earlier must have been mostly the blood it had stolen. We still hadn't really gotten a good look at the thing, but it didn't appear to have a hard shell.

About 20 feet from the road, Fred got caught in some brambles. Julie stayed behind to work him loose while I went on to the car where I planned to deposit the canvas bag inside the reinforced pet carrier.

The long nightmare that had started with Fred noticing something dangerous under the floor was finally coming to an end. Or so I thought.

As I stepped out of the woods, someone suddenly dropped a dark bag over my head and held what felt like the muzzle of a firearm against my belly while someone else pulled my arms behind my back and zip-tied my wrists together. Somewhere in the process, I dropped the canvas bag and its contents.

"Don't say nothin'," a man's voice hissed in my ear, and I was manhandled into what I assumed was the interior of a van. "Face down," the voice said.

I heard Julie call, "Earl? What's going on?"

A few moments later, something small and squirming was dropped on top of me, and the vehicle laid scratch on the pavement as I felt it accelerate into motion.

Was that Fred? Had he gotten loose and come after me, and had my captors grabbed him? Or was it the Rysferatu, still in the canvas bag? I was dealing with a bag of my own, obscuring my vision and my other senses, and the whole experience was disorienting as hell — which, of course, was the intent.

Someone whipped a zip-tie around my ankles and I was pretty much immobilized.

I hoped Julie was all right. And I hoped Fred was still with her. But I had no way of knowing for certain.

CHAPTER 43: CAPTURED

If Fred and Julie had escaped, their next step, I figured, would not be to call the police, but to get hold of Penny instead. She then could summon the troops and launch a raid that would find me, free me and save the day.

Yeah, right.

I had the phone with me. Julie didn't know the number to call, and I had my doubts about Fred. He was smart, sure, and had watched me dial the Marshal on numerous occasions, but could he remember the 10-digit telephone number? And how could he even communicate it to Julie?

I didn't hold much hope for that.

Whatever was squirming on my back was removed, and I didn't know whether to be relieved or scared.

Someone lifted the hood partway up my face, used their fingers to open my mouth and then stuck a straw between my teeth. "Drink this or we kill the dog."

I drank it, feeling a modicum of relief. If they didn't really have Fred, then they didn't know it. If they did have him, then he was going to be held as a hostage pending my cooperation. And I knew they didn't want me dead — not yet, anyway. My family had other plans.

"What did I drink?" I asked after the straw was removed, but before the hood was replaced.

"Roofie."

Great, I thought. I've been given the date rape drug. I'll wake up in the morning with a ferocious hangover and a sore ass, and no memory of what happened.

My apologies to victims of date rape. That wasn't funny. But it was what I thought while I still had an ability to think. Then I thought no more.

CHAPTER 44: HOME AGAIN

Sodium oxybate, also known as gamma hydroxybutyrate (GHB), or Rohypnol — you know, roofies — has gotten a bad rap because it has been used on people without their knowledge. It has no scent, no taste, and when mixed with alcohol the effects can be catastrophic for the victim.

But it's also known as Xyrem, a medication used in the treatment of narcolepsy. Controlled as a dangerous drug by the federal government because of its illegal uses, it can be obtained by legal prescription only by mail order from a single pharmacy that is authorized to produce it. Getting a doctor to prescribe it is like having to prove that you aren't a security risk when being considered for a top secret-level position in the government. You go through a lot of suspicion that you just don't deserve.

How do I know this? My ex had narcolepsy.

When used as prescribed, the drug is mixed with water in two doses. It is not taken until the patient is ready and already sitting up in bed. One dose is taken and the patient almost immediately falls asleep.

Four hours later, give or take, the patient awakens, swallows the second dose, and is back in dreamland until morning.

When it works, it can be very effective. She wasn't sleepy during the day, and the other aspects of narcolepsy — cataplexy, hypnagogic hallucinations and sleep paralysis — you can look them up — all receded into the past as well.

I don't know how long I was asleep, but I'm pretty sure it was hours. If I woke up and was dosed a second time, I don't recall it. They must have had use of a private jet. My family, again.

I awakened with the hood still over my head. My arms were no longer zip-tied behind my back. Instead, they appeared to be strapped down to the arms of a chair.

I moaned, involuntarily, and a moment later the hood was taken off.

The change from darkness to light was as shocking as being dunked in a tank of ice water. Combined with the headache and a sudden onset of nausea, I vomited.

At least I had presence of mind to turn my head, so it didn't splash down my front into my lap. Mostly.

"Oh, dim the lights, wouldja?" I asked.

A familiar laugh came from behind me, and the lights dimmed to a more reasonable level, which in my case was semi-twilight.

"Hi Wilson, or should I say 'Earl'? We've missed you."

He came around to where I could see him. My cousin Angelo, one of the family's enforcers.

"Hi Angie," I said, my voice sounding oddly weak to my ears. "$25 million? Really?"

He laughed again. "Well, that's what we offered to find you, but you know how it is."

"You paid them off with a dollar-fifty in lead."

"Give or take, yeah."

"So I guess you've got something similar in mind for me."

"Not me, no. I've always liked you, Wilson. It was fun growing up with you. It's your dad and The Financier who have plans for you."

"Not surprised. Say, could I get a drink? And a little cleanup here? I'd do it myself, but I don't seem to be going anywhere."

He cleaned up the mess on the floor, wiped my chin, and provided a drink from a water bottle he opened for the first time in front of me, so I could see it hadn't been tampered with. I guess he really did like me.

I felt dizzy, like the drug hadn't worn off yet, and my head hurt and the dim room still seemed awfully bright. At least they hadn't clubbed me unconscious — unlike in the movies, you sometimes don't come back from that, or if you do, your capacity may be considerably diminished.

I remember one guy who was clubbed over the head, to serve as a lesson for a minor infraction. He never woke up from it. Last I heard he was still in a coma, going on 11 years. The family felt so bad about it, The Financier put the man's daughter through college anonymously. She married one of my cousins — one who wasn't involved in the family business.

"What kind of a dog you got, Wilson?" Angelo asked from behind me.

You know how they say in stories that a person's blood ran cold? Now I really knew what it meant. I don't recommend it. Did they have Fred? Did something happen to Julie?

I had to clear my throat before I could speak. "M-my dog? He's a mix," I said. "A little of this, a little of that."

Angelo came over and checked the zip-ties holding my arms to the chair. Still nice and tight, like the ones holding my legs to the chair legs. I wasn't going anywhere.

"I've always liked dogs," he said. "OK if I take yours, after, you know?"

They had Fred? I felt faint. Was he in this room? He hadn't made a sound. Was he all right? I strained at the zip-ties, but there was no give. It was a solid chair.

Be calm, I told myself. This is Angelo, after all. He was a lot of things, but he wasn't an animal abuser. He saved that for people the family wanted to chastise.

I had to clear my throat again, and despite my efforts my voice was shaky. "No offense, Angie, but I can't give him to anyone. He and I pretty much live as equals. If he wants to live with you, it'll be his decision, not mine."

I could tell Angelo was disappointed, even though I couldn't see him, but as he'd said, we'd always gotten along as children. He accepted what I said.

"Any chance you could give me a little slack here? My hands and feet are going to sleep."

"No can do. Your dad tied you up this way, and that's how you'll stay 'til he gets back."

Great, I thought. No double tap in the head for me. They'll want to make it slow and painful.

"Any idea how long that'll take? I'm starting to feel a need to pee."

He didn't say anything, just left the room.

Great.

"Fred? Are you there?" I used his witness protection name rather than the one the family knew. It might confuse anyone listening, and Fred had come to understand that it was his name now.

"Fred? Little buddy?"

Silence. Maybe he wasn't in here with me. Maybe he was somewhere else. Somewhere safe.

I looked around the room. It was familiar. It had one bed now, but back in the day it'd held four. On family get-togethers, we *really* got together. With just one bed now, the room was really spacious — just like all the other rooms in my grandfather's mansion.

Then I heard a rustling sound behind me, of someone or something moving. It sounded low, as if on the floor.

"Fred? Is that you?"

CHAPTER 45: FEAR

Fred and Julie. I pictured them as I had last seen them, back at the wooded area. Fred was caught up in some brambles, and Julie held back to help him get loose, as I went on with the Rysferatu. I'd planned to get it transferred into the pet carrier, and covered with a tarp to keep the light out, then return and help free Fred if he was still stuck.

But I was grabbed and dumped in the van. Something was dropped on me. The Rysferatu? Had I heard Julie's voice before or after that?

They didn't have her. Or at least they didn't take her at that time. There may have been a second crew. Or not.

Angelo hadn't said anything about Julie. If she was being held here, somewhere else in the building, surely he would have said something about it.

He just talked about Fred. Briefly, but still.

He thought they'd grabbed Fred.

Had they? If it was the Rysferatu, it had to still be in the heavy canvas bag. If they'd opened it, or the Rysferatu had managed to get it open, that would have been the first thing Angelo talked about. He wouldn't have been able to talk about anything else if he'd known about it.

I grasped at the mental image of Fred and Julie together, out of danger, as I waited for someone to return. I heard the rustling sound behind me several times, and prayed it was the Rysferatu and not Fred.

If it was the Rysferatu, I wondered how hungry it was getting and what it would feel like to have its teeth or claws rip out my throat as I sat here helplessly in the chair.

I wondered how much of me would be left for the creature to dine on, after my family was done with me. Would I be beaten, pummeled into unconsciousness then awakened to take it all over again? Would I be subjected to small amputations, fingers joint by joint, my toes, my tongue, my eyes? Would my testicles be hooked up to a car battery? Would I be subjected to water-boarding? Bamboo slivers under my fingernails? My eyes held open as I'm forced to watch old family movies on Super 8 film? I'm talking really old here. Pre-VHS tapes. Dark ages stuff.

Here's a possible topic for someone's Ph.D. dissertation: "Which Offers Greater Torture: The Anticipation of Punishment or the Actual Punishment Itself?"

By the time the door opened behind me and someone entered the room, my overloaded bladder voluntarily let loose and I pissed myself. I blame the fear. It would have happened to anyone.

The lights came up to full strength and I blinked as I heard footsteps, breathing, muttered comments, fabric brushing against fabric, the clinking of metal and the clunking of wood, as people entered the room. No one commented on my soaked crotch, despite the sound of dripping that told me I'd left a puddle under the chair.

I was definitely in my old bedroom at my grandfather's house. Why this room? It still had the original wood floor. And it wasn't soundproofed. That room was in the basement. Did they seek familiarity for some reason I had yet to figure out?

About a dozen people crowded in, each lugging a straight-backed chair I figured was similar to what I was tied to, and they formed a two-deep semi-circle in front of me.

Front and center were The Financier and my father. My mother would have been there, but she died several years earlier. But my brother and sister and a number of cousins were present. All grim-faced.

"What is this?" I asked. "An intervention?"

My father's lips twitched as if he found my quip humorous. But just barely so. I had last seen him the night I'd buried River as he'd deliberated whether he was going to make me join her in the shallow grave. There had been no sense of humor that night. I avoided his eyes, not wanting to waste a glare on him.

My grandfather, The Financier, remained sober in demeanor. My father yielded to him, of course.

"Wilson, you disappoint me," the old man said.

"I'm sorry, Grandfather."

"You were caught too easily," he said.

Some of the group looked at him in surprise, as did I.

"I just posted the reward a few days ago, and here you are. I expected it to take at least several months, so I'd be sure and get my money's worth."

"I had something else on my mind," I said.

"I've seen photos," he said. "She is attractive, for a cat lady."

A smile hinted at his lips, then vanished as quickly as it had appeared, like a mouse catching a cat's scent.

"I am also disappointed at your turning state's evidence," he said. "You should have talked to me first."

"Grandfather, I —"

"No, it's too late now, Wilson. You've testified before the federal grand jury. The wheels are rolling and it's taking almost all of the family's resources to keep them from turning any faster," he said.

"Your father and I have been discussing what we should do with you, now that you are back home with your family. If you disappear, there can be no more testimony, and my attorney assures me the case will fall apart. On the other hand, there are particular skills you have that would still be of benefit to the family. Brendan has tried, but he just doesn't have the gift that you have as a cleaner."

Brendan, who was in the second row, nodded his head. Several others did as well. It's nice to be missed. Even in this family.

"You have formed relationships, Wilson, that you knew could be used against you if you crossed the family. I think your father made that abundantly clear when he killed your girlfriend in front of you and made you bury the body."

"Grandfather, that was what made me turn against the family," I protested.

He nodded solemnly. "Your father and I have discussed that as well," he said. "We will not bring it up again."

I was cold where I'd pissed myself, as the urine began to evaporate. At least the dripping had stopped by now, but I could smell the odor rising off my lap.

"We have photos of your current girlfriend, a Julie Evans, I understand. She works at the local zoo as a big cats researcher."

I hung my head, not wanting anyone to read what was reflected in my eyes.

"It would be a shame if something were to happen to her."

I shook my head and looked up at him.

"Oh, don't worry, Wilson, we haven't touched her. Yet. Just know that we could if we wanted to. It would be so easy for her to come into accidental contact with a lion or a tiger in its pen. These tragic accidents do happen from time to time."

My father laughed and a chill ran down my back in competition with the spreading coldness in my lap. I couldn't feel my fingers or toes.

I don't think I've ever felt so helpless in my life, not even when my father murdered River in front of me.

"We don't want you testifying, is that clear?"

"Yes, sir," I said.

"If you refuse to testify, if you recant what you have already told the grand jury, we won't harm a hair of Miss Evans' head," he said.

"I'll go to prison," I said.

"A small price to pay," he said, and this time his lips stretched into a smile. His eyes, though, remained as steely as ever.

"Yes, sir," I said, and hung my head again.

My father cleared his throat.

"Eh? What's that, Son?"

"The dog," he said.

"Ah, yes, the dog," my grandfather said.

"Wilson," he said, "there is one more thing we must ask of you, so you know what harm you have done to the family and are truly sorry."

Figuring what was coming, I shook my head and whispered, "No!"

"Yes," my father said, and he was upon me, cutting the zip-ties that had me bound to the chair, first the arms, then the legs. He put the knife in my numbed fingers. He said, "Kill the dog."

"Grandfather?" I asked, seeking a reprieve. "Please!"

"Kill the dog," The Financier said.

"Kill the dog," my father repeated.

"Kill the dog," my siblings and cousins said.

They all started chanting, "Kill the dog! Kill the dog!" It was like they were at a sporting event, urging on the home team. At least they weren't performing "the wave."

I tried to get out of the chair. My feet and hands were so numb, I dropped the knife and fell to the floor.

I rubbed my hands against each other and shook them out, trying to get circulation going again. Pins and needles, fire and ice shot through my hands and feet as the circulation slowly was restored.

"Kill the dog!" the chant continued. "Kill the dog! Kill the dog!"

I picked up the knife, or tried to. It slid through my fingers several times before I finally was able to grasp it. Even then, it wasn't a firm grip.

I looked at my family. They were all standing, chanting. My father and several others had pistols drawn, in case I decided to come after them with the knife, or in case I refused to kill my dog. You're supposed to love your family; I hated them now with a cold passion.

I finally got turned around to where I could see beyond the chair where I had been confined. There, near the door, on the floor, was a heavy canvas bag. It was moving, its inhabitant clearly conscious and apparently agitated by the chanting in the room.

"Kill the dog! Kill the dog!"

They thought Fred was in the bag.

Who would put a dog in a heavy canvas bag and leave him there? That's just cruel. They should have let him out. At some time while I was knocked out by the roofie and transported across the country, they should have let him out and given him food and water, let him pee and poop, and walked him for exercise!

Not even Angelo had thought of that. Not even Cousin Angelo, who liked me and who liked dogs.

I shambled slowly toward the bag. My feet felt like I was walking on thousands of angry fire ants, all biting and stinging at the same time, every time I put my weight down.

I had the knife in my hand, blade facing forward. I reached the bag and the knife slipped out of my still numb fingers.

"Kill the dog! Kill the dog!" the chant continued. I was really hating my family.

I picked up the knife, then straightened and pulled the canvas bag up with me, reaching for the clips that held its mouth tightly closed.

Behind me was the light switch, a dimmer switch that could be turned to dim the lights, or that just had to be pressed once to cut the lights entirely, bringing total darkness. I staggered backward and hit the switch with my back and at the same time opened the canvas bag and dumped its contents into the room. The stench was immense.

In the sudden darkness, the chanting cut off as if it also had been controlled by the light switch.

I dropped to the floor, turned the bag inside out and pulled it over my head and shoulders, then held my breath.

And prayed.

Muffled by the canvas around my ears, I could still hear screams and gunshots. I felt several bullets hit the door behind me, but I didn't take a hit.

I heard a growling sound, and more screams and more gunshots. Something hit me, hard, and knocked me against the door. My left arm was suddenly numb. But I felt no pain, just shock.

After what seemed a lifetime, the room grew silent except for the sounds of moaning, dripping and sucking.

CHAPTER 46: BLOOD

Even turned inside out, the canvas bag reeked of decayed blood and whatever exotic odor the Rysferatu emitted, and if I hadn't vomited already, I might have done so again. As it is I fought the urge as I stood, feeling around the wall with my right hand for the dimmer switch.

I hit it and turned the lights on again, full strength. The Rysferatu screeched. I pulled the canvas bag off of my head. My left arm was still numb, more so even than when the blood had been cut off.

The Rysferatu continued to screech, then it stopped suddenly and I heard a scratching sound somewhere on the far side of the room, then silence except for a few moans and multiple dripping sounds. It was too bright in there for me to see anything at first, until my eyes could adapt.

I dropped the bag and shielded my eyes from the overhead light. I didn't dare dim the light again, because that might draw the Rysferatu out from wherever it was hiding.

Bodies lay on and under overturned chairs, in a spreading pool that seemed to boil bright red in the light. It looked as if most of my family had been killed, their throats ripped open in the darkness.

Bernard was still alive, clutching his bleeding throat with a bright red hand. Then his hand went limp, and he joined the others in death.

As my vision improved, I scanned the room for the Rysferatu. I didn't see it. There was just the one bed, covered with a bedspread that touched the floor, providing plenty of protection from the light, and I figured the creature had taken refuge under it.

I felt for the door, found the knob, and opened it, darting through and closing it tightly behind me.

The hallway hadn't changed a bit from when I'd prowled it as an adolescent.

I finally looked at my left arm. It was slick and red with blood. One of those final gunshots had gotten me after all. Now that I could see it, it started to hurt.

A phone. I needed to find a phone. There were probably a dozen cell phones in the bedroom, but I wasn't going to go back in there and search the bodies for one.

I then heard a thud and the sound of breaking wood, and a loud voice announcing, "Federal marshals, nobody move!"

I sort of crumpled to the floor, sitting with my back to the closed door, and I covered my bleeding left arm with my right hand, hoping to staunch the flow of blood, waiting for the armed law enforcement agents to find and rescue me on the second floor of the mansion belonging to my grandfather.

CHAPTER 47: SWAT

It didn't take long for the law enforcement agents to clear the first floor and find me waiting for them on the second. Once again, I found myself bound with zip-ties despite my injured arm, this time by the good guys. There were a half dozen of them, decked out in protective vests and helmets and all the other gear you see on SWAT teams in the media, two with weapons pointed at me and the other four ready to continue their search.

"Don't go in there," I told one who was about to enter my former bedroom.

"Shut up," he told me, then he said to another officer, "Get him out of here."

He was out of the room again, vomiting in the hallway, before the other officer had gotten me to the stairs.

"Shut the damned door!" I yelled, twisting away from my escort. "And get me U.S. Marshal Penny Ransome!"

"Who the hell are you?" my escort asked.

"I'm the guy you're supposed to be rescuing. And get that damned door closed before it escapes!"

CHAPTER 48: MEN IN SUITS

Ten minutes later, I was sitting at the dining table downstairs, wanting to rub my hands together in an effort to get the blood flowing in them again, but being good and holding still as a paramedic examined my arm. I hate zip-ties.

"Just a flesh wound," he said. "You're lucky." He cleaned the wound and bandaged it. "If it's been a while since you've had a tetanus booster, you might want to get that taken care of."

I thanked him and assured him I would.

Penny Ransome sat across the table from me, flanked on either side by men in suits she did not bother to identify. Behind them stood two of the agents in SWAT gear with weapons ready in case I proved dangerous.

Maybe I was. I'd left a pile of bloody bodies in a room upstairs, even with a bloodied arm of my own.

"Tell me what happened," she said.

I looked at the men in suits. "How much do they know?"

"Enough," she said.

"The Rysferatu," I started, then seeing the puzzled expressions on the men's faces, I explained, "that's the name I've given the creature upstairs. You know, the vampire that isn't a vampire."

They still looked puzzled. Well, actually one looked incredulous.

"I thought you said they knew enough," I told Penny.

"I'll fill them in, later," she said. "You're just talking to me right now."

I shrugged, and winced at the pain. "Sorry guys. OK, I was brought here with a hood over my head, after being slipped a roofie to knock me out. I had captured the Rysferatu, and when I was grabbed, the idiots assumed it was my dog and brought it along to hold over me.

"In a nutshell, my family wanted me to recant my testimony, serve a few years in prison, then come back to work as a cleaner. They threatened to harm Julie if I didn't, and as punishment for my turning against the family, they wanted me to kill my dog."

I shook my head. "I might not have done this, if they hadn't made these threats. I turned the Rysferatu loose on them."

One of the men in protective gear glanced overhead. He was the one I'd told not to go into the room. "That Rice ... whatever, did that?" he asked.

"Shut up," Penny and I said at the same time. I don't know about her, but I felt a certain level of satisfaction at doing so. A pity I couldn't tell someone to get him out of there as well.

"Continue," she said to me. "How did you get out alive?"

"I'd captured this thing in a thick canvas bag," I said. "I turned it loose, and as I did so I turned off the lights and pulled the bag over my head and shoulders. I figured it must have been starving. Turned loose, it went after exposed throats. That pretty much describes everyone else in the room who wasn't me, since I was protected by the canvas. Before it could turn its attention to me, I switched the lights back on and it sought refuge in the shadows, which I believe were darkest under the bed."

"It's still alive in there?"

"Far as I know," I said. "Not that I've wanted to go back in there to find out, but I've been kind of tied up here."

She and the men in suits stood up, went over to the doorway together and spoke to each other in low voices. A time or two, one of the nameless men looked over his shoulder at me, then turned back to the mumbled conversation.

I looked up at the two remaining agents in protective gear and shrugged again with just my right shoulder. "Everybody has secrets," I said.

They said nothing.

I heard a voice come from the foyer: "Is he safe? Let me in there!" It was Julie's voice.

I heard Fred bark and a moment later he streaked into the room and up into my lap, squirming and wiggling and trying to lick my face, just like the dogs we've seen in the videos when their owners returned from long absences overseas. I hugged him tight, and a moment later Julie was in the room and we all three hugged.

CHAPTER 49: ESCAPE

A short time later, after I'd found an old pair of jeans to replace my damp ones, Julie, Fred and I had been given some privacy in the library and I told them what had happened to me and to my family upstairs.

"And how did you get here?" I finally asked.

"I got Fred loose from the brambles and we were coming out of the woods when I saw the van and several men wearing masks," she said. "They threw something into the van, slid the door shut and drove away. By the time Fred and I got out there, they were gone.

"They slashed the tires of my car, so I couldn't follow," she said.

"Bad," Fred said. "Bad-bad."

"That's right, Fred," she said.

"Anyway, after what you'd told me about the reward, I figured someone had followed us and grabbed you. Fred helped me call Penny."

"Fred, you knew the number?"

"Nuh," he said.

"No, but he'd seen you dial it often enough, he was able to tell me where to press my fingers and in what order. You're right, Earl, this wonderful guy is really smart!"

I hugged him again, favoring my injured arm. He licked my face.

"Penny sent agents to take Fred and me into protective custody while she got things started here. She kept us posted throughout.

"She put this house under surveillance and after it was determined the family activity warranted action by the U.S. Marshals Service, she got a search warrant from a judge who's had no dealings with your grandfather."

"That's harder than you might think," I said.

"Meanwhile, she had Fred and me flown out here. Well, it was pretty much at my insistence. I understand they launched the raid while Fred and I were being brought in from the airport. So here we are."

"I'm glad you're here, both of you," I said. "I was afraid I'd never see you again."

With a sharp knock on the door, Penny swung it open and entered the room, closing it firmly behind her.

"We have a problem," she said.

"The Rysferatu," I said.

"Yeah, that," she said, refusing to use the name Julie and I had given it.

"It escaped," I guessed.

Penny nodded. "It chewed a hole in the wall while under the bed."

"It's in the walls!" Julie said.

"Apparently," Penny said.

"No," I said. "It's long gone. That thing may just be an animal, but it's smart. As smart as it is deadly. It's found a way out of the house, just as it did everywhere else it's been."

"One other thing you ought to know," Penny said. "Not everyone upstairs is dead."

CHAPTER 50: FAMILY MATTERS

I'd guessed it myself, earlier, when speculating about the Anderson family, the victims of the Rysferatu I'd discovered just eight houses down from my own. It had been there for several days, judging from the accumulating newspapers and mail, and the trash container that had never been brought back from the curb.

"It stung them, paralyzing them," I said. And now the creature was loose again. But that was a problem we could set aside for the moment.

Penny nodded, frowning. Nobody likes having the punch line revealed before they're ready.

I asked, "Do you know who survived?"

"We aren't certain if any will survive. It depends on the paralyzing agent this thing used on them. If we can't find an antidote, and if it doesn't wear off, they may be paralyzed for life."

"Let me rephrase my question then," I said. "Who isn't absolutely, positively dead?"

"Your grandfather, for one," she said. "Your father. Your brother, Ike. Your cousins Angelo, Ricardo and Lacey. Maybe one or two others. It was hard to tell with all the blood."

She said everyone was transported to a local hospital where they would be sorted out. Naturally, it was a hospital with a wing named after my grandfather, who was a major donor.

"So what happens to us now?" Julie asked.

"We'd like you to stay in town for the time being," Penny said. "We'll put you up in a safe house, where you'll have round-the-clock protection."

I shook my head. "Anywhere around here would be too exposed. Too much chance someone on the family payroll would be able to reach us, whether it's in a safe house, a hotel room or an agent's spare bedroom."

"What's your alternative?" she asked. "Stay here?"

"Yes," I said. "I know this house. I practically grew up in it. And I know the staff. They're loyal to whoever's in charge and, considering the status of the rest of my family, that would be me."

"Are you kidding?" Julie asked.

Even Fred was staring at me like I'd lost my mind.

"Look," I said. "My grandfather turned this place into a virtual fortress. Video cameras, walls, armed security, the works."

"We got in," Penny said.

"Yes, you did, and without any trouble, right?"

She nodded. "We identified ourselves and they let us right in. No resistance at all."

"That's my grandfather's influence," I said. "He may be a robber baron, all right, but he has a front to maintain.

"This house has hosted high-ranking officials and celebrities. Honest people who wouldn't be caught dead walking into a criminal kingpin's lair, especially if there was a chance of being photographed doing so. Look at the photos on the wall there: That's my grandfather posing with Richard Nixon, heck, all the presidents since then except for Jimmy Carter, and John Wayne, Donald Trump and his father, Arnold Schwarzenegger, Jane Fonda — you get the picture. He has a lot more of these photos in storage, and tends to rotate them in and out on a whim.

"This house is staffed with people who pass a security clearance just as strenuous as that of the White House, and the security people are all employed by an outside company that has no connection to my family except for the contract to work here. My grandfather didn't want to foster a coup d'etat by employing family members as security, and this was his solution."

Someone knocked at the door at this point. Penny went over to see what they wanted, and in a moment returned with a puzzled look on her face and said, "You've got a Skype call."

"I've sort of been expecting it," I said.

Under the wall of photos, beside the circular staircase, was my grandfather's desk — he still used the library as his office after all these years — and on the desk was a laptop. I opened it and switched it on — there was no password — then launched Skype.

Within a minute I found myself looking at two familiar faces: My ex-wife, calling from Thailand, and my father's oldest brother, calling from Washington.

"So it's true," Rebecca said. "You're back."

"You might say that. How's Uncle Ray?"

"He's down with the flu, but he said to say hi."

Then my Uncle Jack spoke up: "What's happened? I heard there was a raid on the old man's place and they carried out a dozen bodies."

Penny stepped up beside me, into view of the laptop's camera. "Senator," she said, although it's been years since my uncle had held that office, "I am U.S. Marshal Penny Ransome and I led the raid on your father's home. The raid was peaceful, without a shot fired, but when we entered the home your father, brother and several other family members already had been incapacitated. Frankly, we are still sorting out who is dead and who is not."

Clearly my uncle had already heard this. As a former senator, ambassador and lobbyist, he had his sources.

"So, Nephew, a coup?"

"No, sir, not exactly. You might call it an intervention that went bad," I said. "I can't really explain it now, but I am the only family member in the house left standing."

Rebecca grinned. "To think I was married to Michael Corleone and I gave him up."

"Stop that, 'Becca!" I said. "This isn't *The Godfather* and I'm not taking over the family business."

"Why not?" my uncle said. "I don't want it, and Ray can't return to the States. The old man told me you were the sharpest of his grandsons, and probably the best to inherit — and I agree. My kids would just screw everything up. Besides, you know where the bodies are buried ..."

He paused, and seemed to remember he was also speaking to a U.S. Marshal. "Metaphorically speaking, of course," he said. "I know your concerns and I'm sure some sort of accommodation could be reached concerning the, ah, less savory aspects of the job."

I shook my head. "It isn't that easy."

"Of course it isn't," he said. "Just think about what I said and we'll talk again soon. Nice meeting you, Marshal."

"Likewise," Penny said, and my uncle logged off of Skype.

"Ray feels the same way, Wilson," Rebecca said. "He said you've always been the responsible one."

"You didn't think so when you left me," I said.

She shrugged. "You were different then. I was different. We all change. Think about it, Willie. Oh, by the way, I like the beard; it's a good look for you." And she also logged off Skype.

I shut off the computer and closed the laptop.

"'Willie'?" Julie said.

"My name is Earl Carter. Willie died a long time ago."

CHAPTER 51: OPPORTUNITY

Later that evening, Julie, Fred and I were in the library again. It was my favorite room in the place, where I'd spent many an hour curled up with a book while a child. It smelled of old books and furniture polish. The old man didn't allow smoking ever since he'd given up the habit himself.

The federal agents were all gone, even Penny, who had been reluctant to let us stay here, but obviously I got my way. My old bedroom was sealed shut with evidence tape, but we had free access to the rest of the house, and I'd spent some time showing Julie around. She especially liked the conservatory, which was currently sporting a desert habitat, with lots of sand, cacti, lizards and a few other denizens of the hot and dry parts of the world. We didn't see any, but I suspected there were snakes and scorpions present as well. Julie was certain she'd seen the paw print of a mountain lion in one patch of sand. I didn't argue.

Fred had done his own rounds, searching for signs the Rysferatu might still have been in the building. He returned with news it was, indeed, no longer present. He made no reference to cats.

Meanwhile, the house staff were professional and agreeable to the change in management. A number of them had known me when I was that child curled up with a book in the library.

The security personnel also were back on duty, and assured Penny and us that all of the mansion's defenses were set up and we would be safe from any would-be intruders — unless they were federal agents, of course. They didn't know about the Rysferatu; it was need-to-know, and I didn't think they needed to know. It likely would not be back.

"So what are you going to do, Earl?" Julie asked.

Fred was lying beside me, enjoying a belly rub, but his eyes were on mine and I could tell he was wondering the same thing.

I cleared my throat. "This is crazy, you know? I've gone from hunting a blood-sucking monster and hiding from crazed killers to suddenly being offered the keys of the kingdom."

"Crazy things do happen," Julie insisted. "You captured the monster and you vanquished the 'crazed killers,' and isn't this what happens in all the classic stories? You win the girl and the kingdom?"

"The monster escaped and is still at large," I pointed out.

"An opportunity for a sequel," she said.

I couldn't help but laugh. "Well, when you put it that way ... but the king is still alive. My grandfather, my father, Ike, my brother, and my cousins, Lacey, Gina, Angelo and Ricardo ..."

"That isn't what Penny said, Earl. They aren't dead, but that thing stung them, and Gina was hit by one of those bullets that were flying around, too," Julie said. "They may never come out of the paralysis, and even if they do, they face charges of kidnapping, extortion, racketeering and so many other federal crimes they'll be put away forever. And that's if they don't get the death penalty, since people died in the process of the kidnapping."

"I don't think that's likely," I said.

Fred closed his eyes, clearly concentrating on the belly rub.

CHAPTER 52: VICTIMIZATION

I remembered the time in the library with my grandfather and the would-be computer geniuses, and I told Julie, stressing the fatal conclusion. "That's the sort of thing I grew up with," I said.

"How awful!"

"I had no idea I was being groomed. Thinking about that, years later, I realized Grandfather chose to bring those two into the library, knowing I was in there. It was intended as a learning opportunity. And I learned."

"Were you involved in the wreck?"

"No. I was still too young to be that involved in the family business."

"Talk about the elephant in the room," she said.

"Elephant?"

"You know, the family business. That woman on Skype — your ex-wife? — she called you 'Michael Corleone.'"

I rolled my eyes.

"No, seriously, Earl. This is your opportunity to take over the family business and do something good with it. Forgive debts, drop all criminal activity, forge a new life without all that baggage from the past."

"That's easier said than done. The federal criminal investigation ..."

"Could be dropped at an instant's notice if you talk to the right people, and you know it."

I stared at her, horrified at the suggestion. Use the family's connections and power to sway the justice system? That's something I had tried to push behind me and I wasn't at all sure I wanted it to catch up again.

"No, that's not what I meant to say," she said. "Look, the people you were testifying against are all incapacitated, right?"

"At the moment, yes. Dead or paralyzed."

"It's as if the Rysferatu did you a huge favor. You don't really have anything to fear from them anymore. You've testified to the federal grand jury already, fulfilling your obligation, right?"

"Sure, until it comes to trial."

"If there is a trial. Right now, no one at that hospital is capable of mounting a defense in a court of law. In other words, no trial. And if it were to come to that, there's also a little matter of a conspiracy to commit a kidnapping, plus the murders of those who actually carried out the kidnapping, to eliminate witnesses that could point back to your family.

"Your own situation could just go away, because you are now a victim, not a perpetrator."

I shook my head. "I don't know ..."

"What was it your grandfather said? 'I'm not twisting your arm to take this offer. It doesn't expire the minute you walk out the door. You can come back any time, or never. I leave it entirely up to you.'"

CHAPTER 53: CLEAN SLATE

The next day, Penny stopped by the mansion. "You'll be interested to know your creature wasn't responsible for all of the blood spilled yesterday."

We were outside, strolling the grounds with Fred getting all the exercise he wanted. It was a beautiful spring day, having rained the night before, and it smelled fresh and breezy. The sun felt good on our faces.

She continued: "Eleven shots were fired. We found bullet holes all over the bedroom, and your brother Roosevelt was killed when a bullet severed his spine, and you already know Gina was also struck by a round. We've linked those two bullets to pistols fired by your father and your grandfather."

I nodded. "So they are directly responsible for deaths that occurred during the commission of a felony."

"That's right," she said.

"So you don't really need my testimony anymore."

"Not really, no," she said.

"Am I about to be arrested? Charged?"

She shook her head. "No. You held up your side of the bargain and, frankly, you've also brought to our attention a serious threat to the safety and well-being of thousands, if not millions."

"The Rysferatu," I said.

"Yeah. That."

"But there's more, isn't there?"

"I don't know what you mean."

"Sure you do. Regardless of what happens to it, my assistance with the Rysferatu is going to be buried so deep not even dedicated archeologists will be able to dig it up. It'll be as if it never happened, and there's no sense in 'rewarding' me for something that never happened."

"Well, it really isn't for me to say."

"Penny, despite what you've sometimes thought, I've been honest with you all along. Fred trusts you enough to talk to you. What is it?"

She stopped walking, so we all stopped. She turned and looked at the mansion, up and down, side to side. It was typical for this region, three stories, numerous bedrooms and baths, two kitchens, garage large enough to fit seven vehicles, surrounded by well-groomed landscaping, trees, bushes, flowers, and a large fence topped with surveillance cameras and other security details I'm not going to reveal. I'll just say that land mines are illegal and unethical, and remind you who my family is.

"It isn't for me to say," she said, "but hypothetically speaking, if a certain federal prosecutor happened to think you were going to stay in the family business, and maintain the family connections, it might be nice for you to be owing him a favor as opposed to anyone else owing you a favor. But I didn't say that."

"He wants me to take over?"

"I didn't say that either. But hypothetically speaking, one might see some benefit in that happening."

"Racketeering, extortion, blackmail, human trafficking, drugs — that's all OK?"

"No! Of course not! We would expect you to, shall we say, divest your holdings ... crap! I can't believe I'm talking this way!" Penny said.

She crouched down and gestured to Fred, who came over and jumped into her arms, licking her face. She hugged him, then set him down again and stood.

"Look, the bottom line is you're free to do whatever you want to do. No charges, a clean slate. If you're going to stay in the business, stay within the law. If you can't then keep it on the down low so that we don't have to get involved. This isn't a Get Out of Jail card that you can use any time you want. This is a one-time-only deal. If we have to come back, you'll be going away for a long time."

I nodded. "OK, that I understand. And what if I choose not to participate, but just walk away from this and everything else? No family connections, no power structure, nothing?"

Penny smiled, an expression so rare it lit up her entire face and made her look years younger. "Same deal. You walk, free and clear, and stay out of trouble, and all is forgiven. We get called in, for any reason, and goodbye freedom."

"Witness Security Program?"

"Do you think you really need it anymore?"

This time I examined the mansion, and the grounds, and looked at Fred and at Julie, then turned to Penny. "Probably not. It appears as if the king's abdicated the throne and made me the crown prince — the heir apparent. Whether I want the crown or not."

CHAPTER 54: NEUROTOXINS

The first thing I did was forgive the debts that had been paid back long ago. And I provided refunds for overpayments beyond what would have been charged in a normal interest-based loan.

Admittedly, a lot of the money for that came from the illegal operations that my family had been involved in, but there was no real way to make good on those crimes. Where people had been harmed, I made anonymous donations that, if treated right, could lift them out of whatever circumstances in which they found themselves.

For loans that had not yet been paid back, I made certain the payments were not proving a hardship. In some cases, I forgave the debts. In others, I reduced the amount of money to be paid.

I also set up funds to take care of those family members who — as the public story went — were paralyzed in a bizarre chemical spill, so that they were well cared for as a cure was sought for their illness. Fred and Julie and I visited them, spoke with their caregivers and inspected the level of care given them.

The news wasn't good.

"We've seen something like this in the insect world," one of the researchers working on the case, Dr. Kristyna Hruskova, told us. She was tall and slender, with long blond hair. In another life, she could have been a model. She spoke with a slight European accent I couldn't place.

"What do you mean?" Julie asked.

"You have heard of the robber fly, perhaps?"

We shook our heads.

"The robber fly is one of the horrors of the insect world — although in the garden it is considered beneficial," she said. "It does not sting its prey; it bites, and into the wound it spits saliva. This substance contains neurotoxins, which paralyze the prey, and enzymes that liquefy the internal organs. The robber fly then sucks its victim dry. It does not look like a fly, as such, but can mimic other insects so it can attack them more easily. It is intelligent, for an insect."

"A robber fly," I said.

"Also known as the assassin fly. Like an air-to-air missile, it can take its prey in mid-flight. It is so fast, the victim never knows what hit it."

"Neurotoxins and enzymes," Julie said. "But we aren't talking about insects, are we?"

Dr. Hruskova shook her head. "What we are seeing here is something similar, injected into humans. We believe, at full strength, the effect would have been death within 12 hours."

She looked at me. "In the case of your family, they got smaller doses, but were poisoned nonetheless. We've done what we can to hold the deterioration to a minimum, but it has been an ongoing battle. If they live," she said, then paused, as if trying to find the right words. "If they live, they will never be the same.

"All of their internal organs have been damaged, to varying degrees. Liver, kidneys, heart, lungs, lymph system, bones, you name it, it has been affected."

"So, you're saying it might be better if they did not recover at all, but were allowed to die," I said.

"No, I am not saying that."

"Not in so many words," Julie said. "But their quality of life would suck."

The doctor nodded. "Quality would be minimal."

CHAPTER 55: FRED'S ARGUMENT

Julie, Fred and I didn't say much as we drove home to my grandfather's mansion. My mansion now.

As we were pulling into the drive, I said, "I don't feel guilty."

"No," Julie said. "There is no reason to."

"They brought it on themselves. They don't deserve to die this way, but ..."

"Nobody deserves to die this way," she said.

The driver stopped to let us out at the front door, then drove on around to the back. The door was opened for us, and we entered the house, heading for the library.

"The Rysferatu is still out there," I said.

"It's had time to recover," Julie said, nodding.

Fred barked agreement.

"That," I said, "that I feel guilty about. We should have killed that thing when we had a chance."

"We tried," Julie said.

I nodded. "In the cave. It should have died then, but it didn't."

"We thought we were doing the right thing, capturing it alive," she said.

"And it would have worked, too, if it hadn't been for my family."

Fred barked, and we both looked at him. He spun around, barking, then stopped, staring at us, and barked again.

"You're right, Fred," I said.

Julie gave me a questioning look, so I translated: "Fred said we're not doing the right thing right now. We shouldn't be doing the 'woulda, coulda, shoulda' thing, but instead should be trying to figure out where the Rysferatu went, then hunting it down and killing it."

He barked again, wagging his tail furiously.

"You have a persuasive argument," Julie told him.

"Of course he does!" I said, opening my arms for him to jump into my hug. "He's Fred, the wonder dog!"

Julie got up, fixed us a couple of drinks at my grandfather's bar, then came back and sat next to me. I took a sip, then set the drink down.

"So what do we do now?" she asked.

"We try to get into the mind of a mutant robber fly/tick/vampire whatever and figure out what it is going to do next," I said. "Then be there when it does it, and bring it down."

"OK," she said. "We know it didn't have much time to feed off your family."

"No, so it's got to be hungry still," I said, and took a drink. It burned as it went down, but warmed me up inside.

"It chewed, or clawed, its way into the wall on the second floor, then found a way out of the house," Julie said. "In the daylight."

We looked at Fred. "It did get out, though, right Fred? It's not in the house."

He barked, then, "Nuh. Emp'y."

"Does this place have any hidden passages, any bolt holes or escape tunnels?" Julie asked.

"I spent a good part of my childhood, when here at my grandfather's house, looking for something like that. There's a hidden elevator here in the library, but other than that, I never found anything."

"Yet the Rysferatu found a way through the house from inside the walls," she pointed out.

I gave her a kiss. "You are something, you know that?"

"Yes, I do," she said. "So now what?"

I turned to Fred. "Come on, Fred, let's go hunting!"

CHAPTER 56: TRACING THE MONSTER

Crime scene tape still blocked the entrance to my old bedroom. I looked at Julie, shrugged, then pulled it down and opened the door. The smell of old blood was nauseating, the buzzing of countless flies filled the room, and Julie turned away.

"I'll wait downstairs," she said.

"I don't blame you," I said.

I took a deep breath of hallway air, then followed Fred into the room, closing the door behind me to keep the smell and flies contained.

All the signs of a forensic crime scene investigation that you've seen on television or in the movies were there. Tape and markers and fingerprint dust and so on. Fred and I avoided most of it as much as possible on our way to the bed. It had been pulled away from the wall far enough to expose the hole the Rysferatu escaped through.

I got down to Fred's level on the floor and aimed my flashlight into the hole. The creature had chewed or clawed its way through wallpaper, plaster and lath, gaining access to a space that was only a few inches wide. Hard to believe something large enough to hold gallons of blood at one time would be so small it could fit inside the wall, but I suspected this thing did not have a solid shell, and was very flexible when not full.

Fred squirmed past me, sniffed the hole, sneezed, then gave me one last glance before following the Rysferatu's trail into the wall. He was pretty flexible, too.

"Bark so we can keep track of where you are," I called after him, and he barked.

I exited the room as soon as I could, leaving the stench and flies behind, making a mental note to check with Penny about whether I could clean up the mess and air it out.

Fred barked periodically, and I followed the signal a surprisingly short distance to the nearest bathroom, where Fred emerged from the cabinet under the sink. The bathroom was an interior facility, without windows, and was always in shadow except for when the lights were on. It had been ideal for the Rysferatu's escape.

Fred lifted the lid to the toilet with his nose and barked. It appeared the creature had come this way, and had managed somehow to squirm into the toilet and out through the sewer lines. Like a rat, or a snake. Or some sort of insect-like creature that is mostly blood sack, but with legs and teeth. This thing had seemed larger in the darkness. Perhaps that was when it was gorged with blood — it hadn't had much time to feed before I'd turned the lights back on. It had fit inside the walls; now, it appeared, the damned thing could slide down a toilet as well.

"Good work, Fred!" I said, stroking his back. "Now we know how it got out."

"We just need to know where it went from there," Julie said after I told her what we'd discovered. "I don't suppose it could have drowned ..."

"Probably not," I said. "I think if drowning were an issue, it would have found some other way to escape."

"Where could it have gone?"

I thought for a moment. "The mansion originally had a cesspool, but when city services reached this area, it hooked up to the municipal sewer lines. So I can think of ... hmm ... at least three possibilities: it climbs out someone else's toilet the same way it entered the one here; it goes all the way to the sewage treatment plant; or it finds some other way to leave the sewers, the same way a rat or snake would get in."

"Or it dies down there," she said.

"Or it dies, yes. Then it would end up at the sewage treatment plant regardless. I visited the plant as a Cub Scout — yes, don't say it! My family was active in Scouting — anyway, as I recall, the plant used direct sunlight to help process the effluent. The Rysferatu, if dead, probably burned up in the light, and if alive, would have tried to stay in the dark. We have to assume it's still alive."

Julie nodded. "Of course," she said. "'Hope for the best, expect the worst.'"

"All I can think of, at the moment anyway, is the worst," I said. "It's going to crawl up into someone's house and start this all over again."

Fred barked, then with his mouth picked up my cellphone from where I'd left it on a coffee table and brought it to me. He dropped it in my lap and barked again.

"You're right, Fred," I said, petting him a moment then picking up the phone. "It's time to call in the authorities."

I speed-dialed U.S. Marshal Penny Ransome.

CHAPTER 57: RESPONSIBILITY

Penny did not sound pleased to hear from us. I had her on speaker.

"You aren't going to like what I have to tell you," she said.

"I haven't liked a lot of things you've told me," I said. "But please, go ahead."

"I kicked the problem with your ... creature upstairs." She was still refusing to call it a Rysferatu.

"You mean the Rysferatu?" I asked, innocently. Well, not really so innocently, but still.

"Yes. That. They kicked it back down."

"And?"

"It's your problem."

"My problem!" I repeated. "How is it my problem?"

"You brought it here," she said.

I buried my face in my hands. Julie picked up the conversation:

"He didn't bring it here; he was kidnapped, and his kidnappers grabbed it, too, thinking it was Fred," she said. "If anything, this is the U.S. Marshals Service's problem, since the Rysferatu was inhabiting a house the marshals were using for the witness protection program."

Penny sighed. "I know. I'm on your side, guys. Really! But my hands are tied. The idea is that you discovered it, you tracked it down, you are responsible for bringing it here and for its escape —"

"Hey!" I protested.

"Its escape," she repeated, "and it's best if you just continued your hunt, so you can find this thing and eliminate it, once and for all. The sooner, the better."

"You can't be serious!" I said, and Fred barked.

"This wasn't my idea," she said. "I talked them into providing you some help, but it's limited because they don't want word of this thing getting out. The panic it would cause would be, well, contrary to our interests."

"What sort of help?" Julie asked.

"That remains to be seen. It depends on what you need."

I told her what Julie and I had discussed, about the sewage system and the Rysferatu's possible access to any house served by the sewer lines — which could number in the thousands.

"If this thing is still alive, we will have more victims," I cautioned.

"I understand," she said. "You mentioned the buildup of mail and newspapers at your neighbors' house, when the thing was feeding on them. We can instruct letter carriers and newspaper carriers to watch for these things under the guise of watching out for senior citizens who are no longer able to respond to daily activities."

"That's a start," I said, grudgingly.

"We can also line up anti-terrorism personnel to consider the possibility of, say, trained rats delivering bubonic plague to targeted groups of people, and see if we can identify any likely targets that way."

"Providing plausible excuses for searches, so no one is aware of what is truly going on," I said.

"Exactly."

"That might work," Julie said.

"It's better than us having to do all of that ourselves. Thank you, Penny, that will help."

"If you think of anything else, let me know. We need to find that thing and eliminate it."

"First things first," I said. "Find it, hopefully before it gets too far along. One of these is bad enough. If it manages to reproduce, and there are thousands out there ... humanity might not survive."

CHAPTER 58: THE HUNT RESUMES

Fred was ready to start hunting right away, but it wasn't as easy as we'd had it earlier.

Before, all we had to do was go out for a walk. The houses were close together, each block had sidewalks for pedestrians, and the streets were laid out in a grid of squares and rectangles. Here, we were among mansions set on acres, far enough apart someone could be screaming bloody murder at one and no one, anywhere else, would hear them. Streets, although paved, were bordered with ditches, not curbs, and twisted like snakes in pain. As for sidewalks, they were nonexistent. But there were signs asking horse riders to stay off the lawn ...

I wasn't going to let Fred run off alone to hunt this beast, but there was no way we could attempt it on foot. And my one experience with a horse during childhood had me drawing a line through that possibility as well. Don't ask.

I briefly considered a bicycle, maybe a tandem so Julie could go along as well, but discarded that idea pretty quickly. Too much effort; we needed to be ready, not puffed out exhausted, if we were to handle the Rysferatu.

A motorcycle? Two motorcycles, one with a sidecar? Not really practical either. Julie had never driven one, and it had been years since a buddy showed me how to do it. I'd need training all over again to feel safe on one.

We settled on a convertible. I would drive, Julie would navigate from the passenger seat and Fred would ride in her lap, his head out the window to sniff for the Rysferatu's stink.

We began searching that night, figuring after dark would be a better time to catch a scent, since the bloodsucker wouldn't be outside in the daytime.

A detachment of security guards followed us from a discrete distance in a black SUV, just in case we needed help. They didn't know about the Rysferatu; they were watching for human predators.

It was a Mustang convertible. I loved that car. We put miles on it, just driving around the neighborhood, trying to swing by every mansion in the area, then expanding into the neighborhoods occupied by less-wealthy residents. There, the streets were straighter, and had streetlights and sidewalks, but were far enough away we continued to drive instead of getting out and walking.

No sign of the Rysferatu. Night after night, nothing. Fred was depressed, and Julie and I weren't any happier.

Penny also reported no sightings from her army of volunteers: the letter carriers and newspaper delivery drivers. Mail was being picked up, and newspapers were disappearing from driveways or delivery boxes on a regular basis.

"This isn't getting us anywhere," I finally told Fred and Julie. "We're missing something."

"But what?" Julie asked.

We were in the library again. It was a favorite meeting place, comfortable and cozy.

Fred barked once and ran out of the room. Julie and I looked at each other and we waited for his return. We heard a sound that was suspiciously like a trash container being tipped over in a bathroom, and a moment later Fred trotted back into the room with the cardboard tube of a depleted toilet paper roll in his mouth.

He set it on the coffee table, then ducked down to look into the inside of the tube.

"Toilet paper tube?" Julie asked.

"Not just the tube," I said, "but what he's doing with it."

"Fred is looking through it," she said.

"Exactly! We've hunted all over the area for the Rysferatu, but one place we haven't looked is inside the sewer mains themselves. If it hasn't come out of the sewers, it must still be inside them."

Fred barked.

"Or it's dead," Julie said.

"We can hope," I said. "But in the meantime, we need to get a look inside the sewer mains."

"I'm not going down there!"

I laughed, then: "We don't need to go into the sewers ourselves. There are other ways to do it."

CHAPTER 59: MINUS ONE

"I can't do this anymore," Julie said.

This was after I'd had a little talk with the mayor, and used some techniques I'd learned from my grandfather to sway him to my way of thinking.

The problem was that I couldn't let him know exactly why we wanted him to spend so much money inspecting the sewer mains, when the city had already done so last year. The idea of sewer main inspections is that the frequency of re-examinations depends on the state of the system exposed during the last inspection. If all is well, then the city might be able to wait a decade before spending the money to do it again and, maybe, by that time technology will have advanced enough that it will be a better inspection at a less expensive rate.

Of course, if the inspection turns up a crumbling infrastructure, then additional money has to be spent to maintain or replace what is there. It may be something as simple as running a new pipe inside the old main, providing a new surface for the effluent to flow through, or as complicated as digging up miles of collapsed or overgrown sewer lines and replacing them completely.

Last year's inspection had reassured city fathers that previous work on the sewer mains had held up, and only a few weak spots needed to be addressed. There was no call for another inspection this soon.

I couldn't tell the mayor about the Rysferatu. He either wouldn't believe me, meaning there was no way he would do this, or he would believe me, meaning word would get out and there might be panic in the streets, a sudden and precipitous drop in property values, and innocent heads would roll. Mine, for example.

So I had to apply pressure.

"You know, Mayor, my family has contributed a lot to your campaign fund," I said.

"And it is greatly appreciated," the mayor responded.

"I'd hate to think that, next election, the money would go to support someone else interested in the office of mayor." As I recalled, the figure was in six digits, funneled in such a way that campaign funding laws were not involved.

"That's blackmail!" the mayor exclaimed.

"No, it's extortion," I said. "But let me offer a compromise, something we both might be able to live with. Supposing I could provide you with a valid excuse for running another inspection of the sewer mains, and add as incentive not only payment for 50 percent of the cost of the project, but also a promise that you will be the only candidate my family supports during the next ... say ... two campaigns, no matter what office you might run for."

"A valid reason, plus 50 percent of the cost," the mayor said. "I would need at least that to run it past the council."

"Of course," I said. "I never intended to ask you to do the impossible."

"What possible reason would there be to run the inspection again?"

"Well," I cleared my throat, "say there are rumors that the provider of the casing used to line the interior of the sewer mains may have been sold a defective product with which to manufacture it. Not that it is the vendor's fault, but merely an unfortunate sequence of events that may have resulted in a less-than-satisfactory quality of product being put into use. I'm sure I can provide some documentation that would support your presentation to the council — details which would pass the inspection of anyone with a chemistry background."

"What about your reason for funding half the cost of the project?"

"As a benefactor who would prefer to remain anonymous, let's say I would like to test a new type of adapter for the device used in the inspection. It is a next-generation technique that would not only help determine whether the rumors are true, but also eliminate any doubt about how good the work was."

"And if the work is defective?"

"Then I'm sure it would provide proof enough for the city to sue the vendor for costs of the inspection plus replacement of the faulty lining, if any is found."

The mayor stared at me for a moment. "You're going after the vendor, aren't you? You are just using me and the city."

I just smiled.

The mayor nodded, satisfied. "Show me the documentation, and we'll talk implementation."

After the mayor was shown out, Julie confronted me.

"I *can't* do this anymore," she said, repeating what she had already told me once, only emphasizing the word "can't" a little bit more than she had before.

"Do what?"

"This," she said, spreading her arms to take in everything around her.

"I miss my cats, I miss my research, my job, my home," she said. "And I'm not sure I like what I see you becoming here, in these surroundings, in this ... place. You seemed so different before, when it was just you and Fred and ... and the thing and the zoo."

"Julie, I —"

"No, don't say it. Look, I don't even know what to call you anymore, Earl, or Wilson, or Willie or something else. You were Earl when I met you, but since you've been here you seem to be more and more Wilson and less and less the man I thought I knew.

"I don't know, maybe it's just me. Maybe I'm the freshwater fish that has suddenly found herself swimming in saltwater, surrounded by sharks. I don't feel comfortable here, and I just want to go home."

Maybe I was still feeling the effects of strong-arming the mayor. I'd had to be tough, and set my feelings of empathy aside while dealing with the city official, and I wasn't prepared to put up any sort of defense other than I just didn't want her to go.

That wasn't enough. Julie went home. I paid her plane fare, first class, and arranged for a car to pick her up at the airport on arrival, and I waited by the phone until I got a call confirming that she had made it home safely, without incident.

I won't say I cried. I won't say I wasn't tempted. I missed her, her presence beside me, her smell, her smile, her touch, her warmth in a cold bed.

Fred missed her, too.

I hated who I was, but I couldn't help it. I had to do what I had to do to make certain everything went as it should.

No matter the cost.

Lives were at stake. Julie knew there really wasn't anything she could do, beyond the role she had already played in tracking down and capturing the Rysferatu. So she had stepped out of the picture to give Fred and me room to work.

I just wish it didn't hurt so much.

CHAPTER 60: PUP TALK

Late at night, Fred woke me up, talking to me. I'd needed a little help falling asleep, and had dug into my grandfather's liquor cabinet, so even awake I wasn't fully conscious, which is probably why Fred's conversation was so clear and articulate.

"I miss Julie," he said.

"I miss her too, Fred."

"Even though she smelled like cats."

"Mm-hmm."

"But we can't let missing Julie distract us," he said.

I didn't wonder at how well he was speaking, using words I didn't know he knew. Maybe it was a dream. Maybe it was the different liquors I'd mixed in sampling the liquor cabinet, one bottle after another.

"You have to stay on target," he continued. "We have to stay on target."

"On target," I repeated. My words may have been slurred. Of the two of us, he was doing better at speaking than I was, at this moment.

"If you get this way when Julie leaves, how are you going to act when I am gone?"

"When you're gone?" I woke up a little more at this comment.

"I'm a dog," Fred said. "I don't live as long as you do. And this monster we're hunting is more dangerous than anything I've ever encountered before. I may not survive our next encounter. You have to be ready. If I don't make it, you can't get drunk every night. I don't want to die, thinking I've wasted my time with you."

"Not a waste," I started, then thought about what he'd said. "No, you're not going to die. I won't let it happen."

"Everything dies. No one is immortal. I'm depending on you to be ready when it happens. You have to be sober. I'm counting on you."

"Sober," I said, sleep starting to drag me under again.

"Promise me," Fred said. "Promise!"

"I promise," I said, or at least I think I said it. The words may have come out a sleepy, drunken mess, but Fred said no more that night.

And he didn't mention it in the morning.

But as the sunlight burst uncomfortably through the bedroom windows, I looked him in the eyes and I said, "I promise, Fred. I promise."

He just sat there, wagging his tail.

CHAPTER 61: NEXT STEP

I used family connections to find an expert who could raise enough questions about the quality of the sewer lining that even I began to wonder if I'd stumbled across the truth while spinning a convenient lie.

I also arranged for a sewer main inspection company to place the lowest and best bid to do the work, which meant I ended up paying about three-quarters of the cost instead of just half. But when you have wealth, there is no sense in hoarding it; just spend it to make life better for others.

The inspection apparatus was drawn from the usual technology, then adapted for my purposes. It was a robot that could travel up and down the sewers, either with or against the flow, with video cameras that wirelessly transmitted their signals to a central processing unit. The robot also was armed with a strobe that flashed the entire spectrum of sunlight, as well as quartz lasers that were capable of vaporizing anything that might impede the flow of effluent — presumably that would include any Rysferatu it might encounter.

While waiting on the slow-turning wheel of bureaucracy to recognize the need for further testing, set it up and begin the process, Fred and I continued our nightly trips into the neighborhoods around the family mansion.

Fred didn't understand why Julie was gone. He just knew it didn't look as if she'd be coming back.

I couldn't explain it to him. At least, not the way I understood it. I eventually told him she missed her big cats, and he understood how one might miss one's animal companions — even if they were felines.

He went on missing her anyway.

As did I.

But life went on.

And as far as we could tell, no one died — at least, not as a result of the Rysferatu.

Not yet, anyway.

CHAPTER 62: NEED TO KNOW

How long can this thing go without eating? I asked myself that, and the answer scared me.

So I called my favorite U.S. Marshal.

"We need to keep a watch on any place where people gather together and spend the night. Nursing homes, group homes, abuse shelters, homeless shelters, jails, hospitals, slumber parties, campgrounds, apartment complexes, hotels, motels, under bridges." I paused to draw a breath and Penny interrupted:

"Already on that. I told you, we have an anti-terrorism team set up to study just this sort of attack. They've already thought of these things, and more, and we're taking action on it."

"What sort of action?" I asked. "Not to be combative or anything, I just need to know so I can rest better at night."

She sighed.

"OK, for example, we've suggested to some groups that there is a new species of rat that has been discovered in the area that lurks in the darkness and bites people as they sleep. Our suggestion has been to leave lights on in common areas, and suggesting soft lighting instead of total darkness where people sleep. Nobody wants to be bitten by a rat, and we have had reports of a high degree of compliance."

"That sounds good," I said. "What about places that are less organized? Slumber parties, campgrounds, and so on?"

"That is harder to do," she admitted, "without causing a wholesale panic. We are trying to balance getting the word out without losing control of just what the word is. Through the schools, we have hinted the possibility of prowlers who prey on children when they gather in groups such as slumber parties. If they insist on getting together, we suggest, a responsible adult should be there, in a lighted area, checking on their wellbeing periodically.

"It isn't perfect," she admitted.

"But it's better than doing nothing," I said.

I told her what I had been up to, arranging the closed-circuit scanning of the inside of the sewer mains, using enough light to destroy any egg sacs left by the Rysferatu, assuming it had fed without our noticing and laid its eggs there.

"The scans are to begin first thing in the morning," I said.

She voiced encouragement and wished me luck, then we concluded the phone call.

I turned to Fred, who had been listening. "What do you think, Fred? Do we have everything covered?"

"Nuh!" he huffed. He crawled onto my lap and curled up, seeking comfort, his tail thumping softly. I loved on him awhile, giving him that comfort.

"We can't think of everything, can we, Fred? No matter what we come up with, there is always the possibility that this thing will go in an entirely different direction. We first found it nesting under our house, then it had taken over a house down the street, moved on to a group home where it somehow destroyed the evidence with fire, and then it began a breeding effort first at the zoo then in a wilderness area just outside the zoo.

"We don't know whether we set it back, to where it will be satisfied with a small family, or if it is ready to go on to something much bigger and, frankly, more monstrous."

I looked down at Fred. He was asleep. He had confidence in me, I guess. I wished I shared that confidence.

CHAPTER 63: THE INSPECTION

The sewer inspection went off without a hitch. Multiple robots tackled different segments of the sewer mains at the same time. We told the city it was more efficient this way, but the effort was designed to drive the Rysferatu — if it was still there — to a central location where it could be destroyed. We didn't want to leave any part of the sewer network in the dark, where it could still nest and breed.

It took several days to complete, working night and day. The inspection turned up some bad spots in the repaired sewer mains, justifying the city's expense and vindicating me with the mayor, as well as shoring up the mayor's reputation with the city council. I ended up making money on the deal, although that wasn't my intent.

But there was no sign of the Rysferatu. Best I could tell, it had escaped the sewer mains and was hiding in the darkness somewhere else.

I was afraid the only way we would be able to tell where it went was when the dead bodies started to turn up.

I called Julie to keep her up to date on what we were doing. She was interested, and sympathetic, and missed Fred and me, but she wasn't coming back. She made that clear, and I didn't press the issue.

I was not going to turn into my father, or my grandfather. I was better than that.

Fred and I went farther afield in our searches. We took walks near the convention center, and at the movie theaters, skating centers and bowling alleys. Anywhere that people might gather, we tried to visit, at least to sniff around the outside of the buildings if they were places where Fred wasn't welcome.

There were a lot of places he wasn't welcome. It's tough being a dog.

We checked bars and restaurants, convenience stores and other all-night businesses.

We went down dark alleys in places where even gang members didn't dare go. I wasn't scared of the people; my family reputation preceded me and protected me from threat. When even that wasn't sufficient, Fred's growl and easily bared teeth frequently settled the matter. He wasn't large, but he could appear that way if needed. I chalk it up as another proof of his intelligence. He knew just the way to growl or bark or whine to get a potential assailant's attention and warn him or her away. Usually a him, but there were a couple of … never mind. Better left unsaid.

In any case, we explored a large part of the city I'd grown up in but had never seen before. It gave me ideas for how I could use the money and power I had inherited, once this pressing problem of the Rysferatu was settled.

If it could ever be settled. I was beginning to despair that we would never know what happened to the monster, when all of a sudden it revealed itself once more.

As anticipated, it was in a way we'd never once considered.

CHAPTER 64: MORE VICTIMS

For Fred and me, it began with a phone call at 3 a.m. It was Penny.

"Get dressed and get Fred. I'll meet you at your front door in 20 minutes," she said.

"What's going on?"

"What do you think? We have dead people." She hung up.

I said some words and Fred covered his ears with his paws. "Sorry, Fred!"

We left the house at 3:30 a.m. The night was so still not even birds were singing. No crickets, no sound but a slight breeze tripping through the leaves.

Penny drove us into an area of town Fred and I had not been to, an industrial park that was as dark as if we'd gone out into the country. No street lights, no building lights, not even a flicker as a denizen of the night lit a cigarette. Good Rysferatu country.

I don't know how I missed this area.

Penny turned the corner and suddenly the area was awash with light. Police cars with emergency lights flashing, ambulance with the same, and portable light stations set up, powered off noisy self-contained generators.

When Penny parked the U.S. Marshals' SUV and we got out, she had her badge out and ready in case we were challenged.

There was no need. Police Lt. David Saunders stepped forward, nodded at Penny then looked at me and said, "Hello, Wilson. I was sorry to hear about your dad. How's he doing?"

"Not that well, I'm afraid. The doctors aren't holding out much hope for a recovery."

"Damn shame," he said. "He was a good cop."

The lieutenant didn't know, or else he did know and was just keeping it tight. Penny and I exchanged a glance, but said nothing. There's a time and place for everything, and this wasn't either of them.

"I suppose you're here because of what we found," Saunders said to Penny.

"If you don't mind," she said. "It sounds like something we've come across before."

He shuddered. "If you know anything about what's going on ..."

"We'll have to see first, won't we?"

"Wilson, are you in on this?" he asked me.

"'Fraid so," I said.

"Wilson is serving as a consultant in this matter," Penny said.

"I promise I won't do anything to disturb the crime scene," I said.

Saunders looked at Fred, but said nothing. He just nodded and led the way. We followed.

We entered a warehouse and followed a corridor between boxes stacked on pallets. I kept an eye on Fred. He sniffed around, but didn't sneeze.

The warehouse was dusty. The lights were on, but they were dim in comparison with the police lights outside. Still bright enough to deter the Rysferatu, I was thinking.

"Were these lights on earlier?" I asked.

"No," Saunders said. "We had to get the electricity restored to the building before we could get any light."

He led us to a series of offices in back, built out from the wall of the warehouse, and up a metal stairway to a second level. Fred sneezed, and Penny looked at me. I nodded, but said nothing.

Saunders led the way to a door where a uniformed officer stood guard outside. "They're with me," he said.

"Even the -?"

"Yes, even the dog," he said, gruffly.

I shrugged at the officer and gave him an apologetic smile; he did not meet my eyes, but stared off into the empty warehouse air.

We entered the office, then stopped just inside the doorway.

It was the homeless campsite all over again: A half dozen bodies, pale in the dim light, their throats torn open. A man, a woman, and four children. They looked Hispanic.

Saunders confirmed my suspicion. "A family of undocumented immigrants from Central America somewhere," he said. "Best we can tell, they were squatting here for a while. May have been let off by a coyote — you know, someone who transported them across the border — with nowhere to go, and they ended up here. The warehouse doors weren't locked.

"We have one survivor, a 9-year-old girl who hid on the roof of this office, then went to get help when things quieted down."

"Did she have anything to say about who or what attacked this family?" Penny asked.

"She called it a 'chupacabra.'"

"What's that?" she asked.

"It's a legend that arose some time back after goats were attacked by something that appeared to have drained their blood, in Puerto Rico," I said. I'd been doing my research.

"Wildlife experts say there is no such thing, but people who have had their livestock attacked say otherwise. It's been described as a sort of reptile, with leathery skin and sharp quills running down its back — yet it's also been described as looking kind of like a mangy dog with a pronounced spinal ridge, and larger than normal eyes, teeth and claws."

"Those descriptions don't match," she protested.

"Which is why it is believed to be fictitious," I said.

Fred sneezed, and all living eyes turned toward him.

I set him down and he sniffed around us, not approaching the corpses. He then circled the bodies and went into another room.

"What's back there?" Penny asked.

"Restrooms," Saunders said.

We heard Fred sneeze, then he returned the way he had come.

"It came up through the toilet," I said.

"What did?" Saunders asked.

"Umm, the thing that is definitely not a chupacabra," Penny said.

"But —" Saunders started.

"Remember the TV series, *The X-Files*?" she said.

"Yes."

"You remember what usually happened to police who got too interested in one of the cases?"

"Not really."

"Well, let's just say you don't want to get too interested in this one. Let us take over the case, and you won't have to worry about it."

Saunders looked at the corpses, clearly thinking of the labor, the paperwork and other headaches that would arise from maintaining ownership over the case, and he nodded. "It's all yours, Marshal. What do you need us to do?"

She looked at me. I was, after all, the former cleaner for my family.

"The first thing we probably ought to do is tamp down on the idea that this might be the work of a chupacabra," I said, although I was thinking the term might be particularly apt in this case. "People can't deal with fictional monsters, so let's refer to this as the act of a giant rat from Sumatra. People know rats, they know they can trap them, poison them or call exterminators, so it won't be as likely to stir people up."

"A giant rat of Sumatra," Saunders said. "That sounds familiar somehow."

"It was mentioned by Sherlock Holmes in one of Sir Arthur Conan Doyle's stories," I said.

"That must be it," he said.

"Your forensic people haven't been through the crime scene yet, have they?" Penny asked. Not yet; they'd been waiting on the Feds. Us. "All right, then, I'll need a copy of their findings when they're done. Meanwhile, we'll take care of the disposition of the bodies. What is the status of the survivor?"

"She's with social services right now."

"Very well. We'd like a chance to speak with her later."

"I'm sure that can be arranged," Saunders said. "You may want to have a translator on-site. I'm not sure she knows any English."

"Good to know. Thank you, Lieutenant Saunders."

After a few more instructions, the police detective left us alone at the office. He even pulled the officer at the door away for other duties.

"OK, Fred, let's see if we can find our beastie," I said. He barked, and headed out into the warehouse.

CHAPTER 65: THE WALL

The warehouse was a big place. I was surprised it had so much stuff stored in it, yet appeared to be abandoned.

"Bankruptcy on top of a divorce," Penny explained. "It's been held up in the courts for several years as the various parties try to sort through their differences, and in the meantime everything has just sat here, awaiting settlement. Apparently whatever is in those boxes and crates isn't going to lose any value while it sits here."

Fred led the way down the stairs, then he followed the scent into the stacks. I had my tactical flashlight out, and behind me the marshal was prepared with her pistol.

A lot of time had passed since the Rysferatu escaped down the toilet at my grandfather's mansion. It could have fed any number of times. The discovery of these bodies only confirmed that it still lived and still sought the blood of the living.

"We may not be looking of just one Rysferatu now," I whispered to Penny. "It may have reproduced. If the eggs have hatched, we may be facing dozens, hundreds, I don't know."

"I shouldn't have mentioned *The X-Files*," she said.

"Do you see yourself as Scully, or Mulder?" I asked.

"Neither," she said. "Do you wish you'd called it a chupacabra instead of that stupid name you made up?"

"*Touche'*, Marshal, *touche'*."

Fred sneezed again, which brought us back on track.

He stopped at a stack of unknown inventory next to a side wall, sniffed its base, then went around the corner and out of sight between the stack and the wall. A moment later, he started barking.

"Sounds like he's outside," Penny said.

I shined the flashlight between the stack and the wall. A section of the wall did not reflect the light.

"He's outside, all right," I said.

"Stay there, Fred, and we'll come around!"

He barked again, and the Marshal and I made haste for the nearest exit.

The police were still outside. They watched us go around the building, saying nothing and making no move to follow. I guess when the Feds take over a case, they really take over.

We found Fred waiting for us outside, next to a hole in the wall about the size of a large watermelon. It looked like it had been punched through from the inside by a dwarf with super strength.

"That's a steel wall," Penny said. "How did it get through it?"

I flashed the light on the edges of the hole, then explored the wall of the building on either side of the hole. There was a dent not too far away.

"Looks like a forklift accident. See that dent? The forklift must have hit at an angle, and only one of the forks went through."

"I'll have that checked on," Penny said. "If that creature was able to punch through a steel wall, we may be in for a world of hurt."

Fred barked, reclaiming our attention yet again, then led the way into the darkness between the abandoned buildings.

We followed, aware with every step we took that death lay somewhere in front of us, in the dark.

CHAPTER 66: THE DOCK

It was about this time, I learned later, that my father and grandfather died as a result of the Rysferatu's venomous bite, or sting. The others who also were attacked by the creature did not live much longer.

The two who just suffered gunshot wounds, my cousins Lacey and Merlin, were recovering, although it looked like Lacey would never walk again, and Merlin had to have his left arm amputated. I don't care what they show on TV, gunshot wounds can be devastating for people who suffer them.

My brother, Ike, and my cousins Angelo, Ricardo and Delmont, would soon follow my father and grandfather. We would be holding a huge funeral — but that's still ahead of the story.

It was about 5 a.m. now, and Penny and I continued to follow Fred through the dark industrial park. We came to a waterfront dock, where the trail ended.

"It's on a boat," I said.

"How would it have gotten on a boat?" Penny challenged. "This industrial park has no businesses left. Why would anyone dock here?"

"Anyone doing legal business," I agreed. "But that wouldn't stop someone else. Drugs, a party boat, human trafficking ... the family back there had to get here somehow."

"Whoever it is picked up a hellish cargo."

She pulled out a phone and made a call. Meanwhile, I knelt beside Fred and petted him. He ignored me, and scratched at the rough wooden surface of the dock, whining. I lay down on the dock and stuck my head over the side, shining the flashlight underneath.

What looked like an egg sac seemed to stare back at me accusingly, and I jerked the light away before I could cook it the way the one at the zoo had popped and sizzled.

"Penny," I said, backing away from the edge of the dock. "While you're on the phone, I think we need some help here at the dock."

She summoned a boat along with the helicopter she'd already called in, the latter to search the waterway for any likely nighttime boaters who might, or might not, still be alive.

I didn't know whether the Rysferatu was under the dock or long gone, but I figured researchers would want to have a look at that egg sac, to see if they could learn anything more about the creature that had laid it.

It had to be collected under cover of darkness, of course, not for reasons of secrecy, but just so it would survive collection. Expose it to bright light the same way we had the zoo specimen, and there would be nothing to study.

I checked my cellphone, thinking of messaging Julie to tell her what we'd found, and discovered my phone had no bars of service here.

"How does your phone work here and mine doesn't?" I asked Penny.

"Satellite," she said. Even poorly paid and poorly funded, government agents still had access to better equipment than most civilians.

"I need to get me one of those," I said.

We waited on the dock for the backup personnel Penny had called in. The helicopter, of course, arrived first. Her phone rang, and she explained to the caller what she required the helicopter to do. It sped off, shining a spotlight on the dark expanse of the waterway.

Then we waited for the boat, which took at least another hour to show up. In the meantime, Fred and I patrolled the shoreline, checking to make certain the Rysferatu hadn't doubled back to shore somehow. We came up empty, and returned to Penny as the sky began to brighten in the east. The night was drawing to a close, and that's when the boat pulled up.

"What kind of boat is that?" I asked.

"Top secret," she said. "Designed to handle nuclear, chemical and biological situations in a marine setting. You didn't see it, and you will never tell anyone about it."

Remember all the secrecy that once surrounded the Air Force's stealth bomber? This was that kind of secret. That's all they will allow me to write about it, and it took several months of negotiations and suggestions and cross-proposals to be able to say that much. Maybe when it's been declassified ...

It had a new car smell. I wondered if Elon Musk's engineers had played a role in its design and construction, as I stood briefly upon its deck. If it had a deck. Sorry, can't comment about that, either.

I directed a crew member, who was dressed in head-to-toe hazmat protection, to the egg sac that I'd seen, and it was carefully collected and sealed inside a light-proof container. It was taken from my view and I never saw it again, which was fine with me.

A crew member gave Penny and me eye protection and took Fred out of my view for his own protection, then a device was used to blast the underside of the dock with a light so bright my tactical flashlight would have seemed like a lighted candle next to a spotlight in comparison. Any other egg sacs or the Rysferatu itself could not have survived the onslaught of that torrent of incandescence. In fact, I was surprised the dock didn't instantly ignite in flames, because I could feel the energy of the light being reflected back in my face.

The light went out, and everything was dark. Not even the rising sun could penetrate the goggles. I pulled them off and blinked at the pale red disk as it slowly rose above the horizon.

"Your eyes will adjust in a minute or two," the crew member said, handing Fred back to me.

"Wow!" I said.

"You didn't see that either," Penny said.

"Gotcha!" I said.

We stood on the dock and watched as the boat I never saw sped away, leaving a barely noticeable wake. "Amazing," I said.

"Tell me about it," Penny said. "Oh wait, that's right, you can't. If word about this leaks out ..."

"Solitary confinement for the rest of my life," I said.

"In a black hole somewhere in a foreign country where you will never again hear a word of English spoken," she said. "That goes for you, too, Fred."

He just looked at her and snorted, grinning and wagging his tail.

Penny's phone rang. It was the helicopter, reporting lack of result. If any boat had been on the waterway and visited the dock that night, it was no longer discernible from among the other boats that were now venturing out onto the water with the light of morning.

The Rysferatu had gotten away again.

CHAPTER 67: TO THE STRONGEST

When back within range of a cell tower, my phone registered several messages from the hospital where my family members were patients. I was an orphan, and heir to The Financier's empire for certain now. It was not a pleasant thought. I thought about Julie and wondered if there was any way I could walk away from it.

I made funeral arrangements as Penny made similar arrangements for the family found dead at the warehouse. She left to interview the sole survivor, leaving me to deal with numerous calls of condolence and vows of continued faithfulness as word about The Financier's death got out. She promised to tell me anything she learned from the frightened girl.

My uncle, the former Senator, called me about noon.

"Well, Nephew, it's official," he said. "You are the new Financier."

Crap!

"And if I don't want it?"

"Let me tell you a story. A little more than 2,300 years ago, there was a young man who led an army that whipped every foe it encountered until he had conquered the entire known world. He became the most powerful man of his day, holding together his empire through force of will and a savvy means of leadership that has been all but forgotten in this day and age.

"One day he became ill from some unknown illness, and as he lay on his death bed, his generals asked him who he chose to be his successor. Word is that he said, 'To the strongest.'"

"That was Alexander the Great," I said.

"Yes, and you know what happened to his empire."

"It collapsed without a strong leader to hold it together. His generals warred and squabbled and the empire folded. Only Ptolemy in Egypt managed to hang onto a portion of the conquered lands, starting a dynasty that ended with Cleopatra's death."

"In this family, Wilson, you are the strongest. You are already there, in place, in charge. If you were to leave now, everything your grandfather put together would fall apart — and while I'll admit some of that would be of benefit, far too much of it would result in a type of chaos that would be detrimental not only to the family, but to the thousands of other families that depend on us — on you — for their livelihoods. No one else is capable of holding it together, although I'm sure there are those who would like to try. It has to be you."

It has to be me. Great. I thanked him, told him when the funeral would be, and hung up.

Some people are born to greatness. Others have greatness thrust upon them. As for me, I would just have to do my best and follow my conscience, I guess.

Meanwhile, there was a blood-sucking monster out there that would wreak all sorts of havoc — no matter what my decision — if it wasn't caught and destroyed soon.

Where could it have gone? What could I — what could Fred and I — do to track it down and kill it?

I doubted it was capable of piloting a boat by itself. It would be a silent stowaway, biding its time in the darkness of a hold, perhaps, until the boat docked again and, under cover of night, it could make its escape to find new victims.

Or, if it were less capable of reasoning and more animalistic, it might attack and kill whatever crew was on the boat, and wait helplessly on board until the boat drifted to shore and the creature — again — could escape into the night.

Was it intelligent? Did it learn from its mistakes? Did it plan ahead? Was it smart enough to start a fire to cover its tracks, or was that just an accident? It had seemed pretty smart when it didn't interfere with me as I opened the garage door so it, too, could escape from the neighbors' house.

Yet it had made no apparent effort to chew its way out of the canvas bag that had held it on the way to my grandfather's mansion. It had teeth that could rip out a human throat; surely a canvas bag wouldn't be that difficult. Then again, it had been considerably weakened after being flashed in the cave. Had it bided its time, waiting for the right moment, or did it just take advantage of being freed?

Intelligent? Or acting on instinct? Capable of planning ahead? Or incapable of action when faced with an unusual dilemma? Did it operate from a primal reproductive instinct? Or did it go by a particularly self-sufficient insight that could let it chew its way through a plaster and lath wall and make its escape down a toilet into the sewers?

I had no answers, only questions.

But I suspected there was a boat out there somewhere with a dead crew, floating downstream, or with the tide and current, until it grounded somewhere. Or sank, which might be preferable.

It called to mind the mystery of the *Mary Celeste*, a brigantine merchant ship that was found drifting, apparently abandoned by her crew, off the coast of Portugal in 1872. The sails were set, there was plenty of food and no signs of a struggle, but the lone lifeboat was gone as was every living person known to have been on board.

Would investigators have known to search the vessel for a creature capable of killing everyone? Would anyone finding a modern abandoned vessel know to do that?

Through my connections, I chartered a boat. It was time for Fred and me to set sail.

CHAPTER 68: ON THE WATER

It was just Fred and me on the boat. The owner had offered to come along, but I'd turned him down. I didn't want to risk harm coming to anyone else who wasn't already involved in the hunt. I made sure to equip myself with night-vision goggles. Even though Fred could see well in the darkness, I could not, and I didn't want to give the Rysferatu a chance to sneak up on us.

The boat was considered a yacht, because it was large enough, but it was a trawler class. The interior was fixed up much like you would find a land-going RV to be, except there were more tie-downs and the materials it was remodeled with were less likely to peel, warp or grow mold or mildew in a damp environment.

In addition to the night-vision goggles, my contact had provided tactical gear such as a protective vest, and probably enough firepower to set off alarms at the Bureau of Alcohol, Tobacco, Firearms and Explosives, if they'd known about it. With any luck, no one would have to find out.

I manned the helm, because it was the most logical place for me to be, of course. Fred took the far-forward position at the bow, sniffing the air for any hint of blood-sucker, and we slowly motored downstream.

I didn't know for certain the vessel boarded by the Rysferatu would head downstream and not upstream, but if the creature had killed everyone on board, then downstream would be the logical direction to drift.

I figured the odds were better than 50-50 that we were going the right direction.

We traveled for hours, threading traffic on the waterway, trying not to get in anyone's way and, no doubt, violating some of the rules of the water. So far, though, we had not attracted the attention of the authorities.

Or perhaps we had, and Penny was running interference for us. I hadn't notified her of my intent, but it was entirely likely she'd figured we'd do something stupid like this and smoothed the way.

It's good to have influential friends, isn't it?

Then again, that was my family's stock in trade.

Fred and I watched for any boat that seemed adrift as opposed to traveling under power. We swerved to check a couple of possibilities out, only to find they were busy with other things and not paying that much attention to where they were. I don't want to get too explicit, so let's just say some nudity was involved.

Fred and I docked briefly at a restaurant that served, of course, sea food, then continued our hunt downstream.

I'd lost count the number of boats, skiffs, barges and other vessels we'd passed when, as evening neared, Fred started barking to catch my attention. He assumed the pointer position, body and tail stiff, one leg raised to point the same way his nose was pointed.

It was a small cargo ship, a tramp freighter by appearance, commonly called a coaster because it would hug the shoreline, making stops at ports along the coast. I estimated it at 50 yards long. It was low-slung, with a low pilot house at the stern. I didn't know much about ships, but this one looked ready for the scrap yard. It was already in shadow as the sun appeared to sink away at the edge of the horizon.

I could hear someone shouting, then the shouting was cut off by shrieking, then that, too, was cut off, replaced by a foreboding silence.

Despite the growing shadows, I still could make out the name on the side near the bow. I won't tell you what it was, because there might be some litigation still unresolved. Let's just call it *Scrappy* (seriously, not its real name).

The *Scrappy* did not appear to be under power, but was flowing with the current. Other than the screams, it had not called attention to itself, but Fred indicated he could smell the creature's distinct odor coming from that direction.

I pulled my boat alongside the *Scrappy* and tried to get the attention of anyone who might still be alive on board. There was no response.

I suspected the worst.

Using equipment thoughtfully provided by my contact, I threw hooks over the side of the cargo ship and prepared to board. Fred jumped across before me, so I didn't have to worry about him.

Except I was worried about him. If the Rysferatu were indeed on board the *Scrappy*, Fred and I were both taking a great risk.

I didn't want to call Penny until I knew for certain.

I threw my contact's bag of goodies over, then clambered aboard, feeling almost as if I should have a cutlass in my hand and a patch over one eye, with twists of smoldering cannon fuses tied into my beard. A pirate's life for me, aye matey?

Yelling to catch someone's attention, despite the screams still uncertain as to the fate of the crew, I made my way to the pilot house. I brought the bag of goodies with me.

The pilot house was empty. I could see the engines had been powered down and the wheel locked in place, so I figured it had been abandoned intentionally. Had the officer on watch gone in search of the others when his replacement failed to show up, and no one answered the intercom? Temporarily leaving one's post had to be an option when something appeared to be going wrong, right?

Fred and I stepped out and made our way down to the lower deck. I was reaching for the closed hatch when I heard a voice.

"No, *señor*, don't go in there! Chupacabra!"

A teenage boy was looking at us from around the corner of the superstructure.

"Where is everyone?" I asked.

"*Muertos* — they are all dead, *señor*."

"Are you part of the crew?"

"No, *señor*. I am *el polizon*, a stowaway."

"You were with everyone back at the warehouse, weren't you?"

He looked down. I could see he was crying, but I said nothing. "All *muertos*," he said. "Chupacabra was there, too."

"Not everyone. I'm told a girl survived."

"Rosalita?"

"I don't know if that's her name. I didn't see her. I was just told that a girl survived, and she's safe. Can you tell me what happened? Wait — hold that thought," I said. After all, we were on a ship with a chupacabra, or Rysferatu, on board, and the sun was already below the horizon. It had been a beautiful sunset, but the scary part was about to begin.

"Where is the Rys — uh — chupacabra now?"

"I am not sure, *señor*. I have been hiding."

"OK, here's a flashlight," I said, handing him my tactical flashlight. "Turn it on and shine it around you. The chupacabra doesn't like light."

I then reached into the bag of goodies and pulled out a handheld magnesium flare. It was simple to use: Just pull one end away from the other so it telescopes out, until it clicks into place. There's a cap on the end that you have to unscrew, then a tab attached to a cord, which you pull out. This ignites the flare, and in a couple of seconds, the plug at the end is ejected, and the magnesium inside begins to burn at 2,000 degrees, kicking out up to 10,000 candelas of light.

Now, how does 10,000 candelas compare with the 2,000 Lumens of light my tactical flashlight produced? I'm glad you asked.

A candela is a measurement of light produced by a source. For example a single candela is about the same brightness as a single candle produces.

A lumen is a measurement of how much light is given off by the source.

What's the difference? I read somewhere a laser pointer, for example, could have a low lumen value, but a high candela rating, because while it doesn't give off much light, it can be seen from a long distance away.

So a 10,000 candela flare is very, very bright, but from where I was standing, my eyes partly shielded from the flare by my hand and arm, the lumens were lower. In front of the flare, however, it's like daylight.

For 60 seconds, then the flare goes out and darkness swoops in like an owl on an unwary mouse.

Fred and I were going to have to work very quickly.

CHAPTER 69: DEATH SHIP

With the flare sputtering into life, I swung open the hatch and Fred jumped through the opening. I followed, pulling the hatch closed behind us. We were in a passageway, illuminated only by the flare, which was throwing off a lot of smoke as well as the bright light. Midway down the passageway, I saw a body crumpled on the deck.

As I got close, I saw it was the corpse of a man, and it looked as if his throat had been torn open. He lay in a pool of blood — the creature had killed him, but hadn't fed.

And the flare went out.

Fred barked, and I yanked another one out of the bag by feel, extended the tube, removed the cap and pulled the tab. Seconds that lasted way too long went by before the flare burst into bright life. I pulled several more out of the bag so I wouldn't have to go hunting for them when this one went dark.

"We've got to hurry, Fred," I said.

He sniffed around the passageway, running back and forth, then stopped at a door that appeared to be ajar. Holding the flare in front of me, I pushed at the door and it swung open.

There was the rest of the crew. They were in the galley. It looked like they might have been eating, or resting up before going on duty, when the Rysferatu attacked. Not one of them moved.

The flare sputtered, and I had another one out and throwing 10,000 candelas of light before the other one died.

"Is it in here, Fred?"

"Nuh," he said. He went back to the door and looked out in the passageway.

"Damn it!" I said. "We aren't going to find it with this much light. Fred, I'm going to have to go dark."

He glanced back at me, then went out into the passageway.

I took a quick look at the crew while there was still light. It didn't look like any one of them was still breathing.

The flare died, and I closed my eyes, willing them to adjust to the darkness, and pulled the night-vision goggles over my face, settling them in place over my eyes. When I opened my eyes again, they still hadn't fully adjusted, but I could see well enough to avoid the bodies on my way back to the door.

I reminded myself, if I were to light another flare, I needed to remove the goggles before doing so if I didn't want to be blinded.

Fred was down near the end of the passageway, staring at another hatch that was ajar. I joined him there, nudged the hatch all the way open and found access to a lower deck.

"Down there, huh?"

He huffed, then led the way below.

I started to follow him, thinking what a fool I was for doing this. My family had profited from getting other people to do things for us. And this wasn't my job. I should have called Penny, and there should have been an entire squad of SWAT officers or the Marines or a SEAL Team descending between decks, not just Fred and me.

But here we were. I froze at the hatch, my thoughts locked in a cycle that would not, could not be ignored.

Below us was the Rysferatu, a creature whose only desire — I figured — was to live and reproduce. Had it managed to do that without killing my neighbors down the street, or the people in the group home, or the homeless people camped behind the zoo, or the immigrants just desiring a better home for themselves — I wasn't going to begrudge the thing for the swath it cut through my family, nor through the crew of this vessel who were likely up to no good — if it had just acted like a regular tick or whatever base creature served as the origin model for this thing, then Fred and I wouldn't be here, hunting it down on a drifting ship crewed by the dead.

Even now, I supposed, I could turn around and walk away. No one would blame me, or think any less of me than they already did — except for Fred.

Fred would know. Fred would look at me, would peer into my soul, and he would know. He might not judge — dogs are good at that — but I would know that he knew.

I smelled old cooking odors, sweat, cigarette smoke, mold and mildew, diesel fuel and something else. Not fresh paint — these bulkheads had not seen fresh paint in years, perhaps decades. No, it was something rotten. Something bloody. Something that made me want to pee my pants; but I didn't.

I still hesitated. I needed a trigger, something to kick my temporary paralysis to the side and get me moving again.

Fred sneezed, down there in the darkness. That was all it took.

We reached the bottom deck. The hatch was open into even more darkness.

Fred paused at the doorway, then backed away.

"Bad," he said. "Bad-bad."

CHAPTER 70: FOOL IN THE DARK

For me, everything was a dim green, diminishing into darkness. "Is this the hold?" I asked, whispering. I saw barrels. Barrels stacked on barrels, fading green into black the farther away they were.

This wasn't a big ship. It was strictly for coastal freight, so it wasn't built to hold millions of gallons of fuel oil. And considering the rust and mildew and overall condition of the vessel, I had the impression this cargo wasn't necessarily registered on any official documentation for origination or destination ports.

But there were a lot of barrels in there. Each holding 55 gallons of something that was worth transporting from one abandoned dock to another, without involving any more maritime authorities than necessary.

And somewhere in that darkness was death.

I know what I should have done. Hindsight has its strengths, but its major weakness is that it isn't foresight.

I should have shut the hatch, dogged it down and retreated with Fred. We could have taken the young man waiting for us on the main deck, and we could have returned to my borrowed boat and called Penny and waited for the cavalry to come and take over this operation.

I was an amateur, in way over my head. I was a fool. A fool in the dark.

I squatted there just inside the hatch, spread open the bag of tricks in front of me, reached in and pulled out a flare.

Remembering what I'd warned myself about earlier, I pulled the night-vision goggles away from my eyes, and blinked blindly at the resulting darkness.

"Bright light coming, Fred," I said. "Watch your eyes."

I extended the tube. I twisted off the cap. I grabbed the tab and pulled it. And waited for the chemical processes inside the flare to follow through, igniting the magnesium mixture and throwing off the full 10,000 candelas of light, burning at 2,000 degrees for 60 amazingly brief seconds.

Waiting...

Fred barked. No, he howled, and he jumped onto me, first my bent knee then up my chest, just as he had climbed the cliff to the caves what seemed a lifetime ago already. I smelled the most disgusting odor then, and something hit me in the face.

And of course the inevitable finally happened. The ship, left unmanned, without lookout, without human guidance, without engines throbbing to propel it through the water so the rudder could do its job even while locked down, ran into something. A sandbar, I learned later. At least it wasn't another boat.

At the same time, Fred screamed, and I, already off-balance what with his suddenly climbing me, and the ship shuddering to a sudden stop, and something hitting me in the face like a piece of thrown garbage, I fell over. I dropped the flare. I was swept with a feeling of utter doom and despair.

I heard crashing sounds, like cargo shifting, tipping over, falling to the metal floor. The smell of fuel oil grew stronger.

Light came on, as the flare finally burst into brilliance.

It was inside the bag of goodies, there with all of the other flares, and ammunition, and explosives. Light that would have measured 10,000 candelas if I'd had a way of measuring it lit up the bag like a Jack-o'-lantern made of nylon on Halloween, exposing the contents to 2,000-degree heat.

I said something. I don't remember exactly what it was, but you have a good imagination. I'm sure you can figure out what you would have said in that situation.

I got up. Where's Fred? There he is! He's just lying there, not moving. I said something else, but whatever I said was drowned out by horrifying shrieks.

Beyond Fred I saw the Rysferatu, caught in the bright light now coming from the bag.

It didn't look like a Nosferatu after all. I'd only caught a glimpse in the dark, and my imagination had put a face on something that was too horrible to contemplate. The face, more insectlike than mammal, burst into flame in the bright light and was gone.

I grabbed up Fred's limp body, turned and rushed topside.

That bag of tricks was about to pull a really big trick on this ship, and I didn't want to be anywhere near it when it did.

Up to the main deck, with a frighteningly bright illumination guiding my climb from below, and down the still-dark passageway, I flung the hatch at the end open and felt the fresh night air against my face.

The teenager was there, shining the flashlight in my eyes.

"Run!" I said. "My boat!" I pointed, and we raced across the deck of the ship. I expected it to rupture at any moment, blowing burning fuel oil and pieces of shrapnel into the air, vaporizing us puny humans as we crawled across the top of the floating bomb.

The teen beat me to the boat, and jumped down into it. I handed Fred's limp body to him, then followed, cutting through the ropes that held us fast to the side of the *Scrappy*.

"Go below," I said. "Cover your ears with your hands and open your mouth. Breathe through your mouth. Go!"

He disappeared into the cabin below the waterline, and I switched on the engine and powered the little boat away from the big one. Fortunately, the boat did not ride as low in the water as the coaster, and it was not mired on top of the sandbar.

We got maybe 50 feet away from the ship when it split the night with a tremendous roar and towering fireball that had to be visible from miles away.

I ducked low as pieces of ship hit us like shrapnel. I wouldn't be returning this boat in the same shape as it was when I borrowed it. Something hit my forehead, but I shrugged it off.

Pieces of the ship that had been blasted into the sky rained down on the waterway, and us. Some of it was burning. I was thinking about hunting up a fire extinguisher when one piece of debris fell from the sky, smashed through the wooden deck and disappeared below.

A moment later, the teenager climbed up from below and said, "*Señor*, water is coming in. I think we are sinking."

He still had Fred in his arms. The debris from the ship stopped falling, and what remained of the old tramp freighter now just burned.

In the light from the fire, I opened the locker where life jackets were kept, then took Fred from him as he put one on. "What is your name?" I asked him.

"Paco," he said. His eyes were opened wide as he stared at me. I wondered how well he understood what was happening.

"All right, Paco, I think we're going to have to swim for it. Even if you can't swim —"

"I can swim, *Señor*."

"– the life jacket will keep you afloat until you reach land or are rescued."

He nodded, and took Fred again so I could shrug a larger life jacket on. I then took Fred's limp body back. "You ready?"

Still staring at me, he nodded again, then jumped into the water. He didn't drop far; the boat was sinking rapidly.

I followed him into the icy water, holding Fred close to me, making certain his head stayed up in the air. I couldn't tell if he was alive or dead. But I had to stay alive if he was to have a chance.

My hands were full. I couldn't swim, but I could kick my legs. I felt a hand on the back of my head, then it latched onto the back of my life jacket. "I will help, *Señor*!" Paco said, and as he held onto me with one hand, he stroked with the other and kicked his legs as well.

We reached shore that way. Paco climbed out first, then he helped me. I was so tired, so physically exhausted, I had trouble making my legs work to climb out of the water.

Paco still had the tactical flashlight, and he switched it on. "Your dog, *Señor* ..."

I sat on the ground and set Fred in my lap, and checked his limp body as Paco held the light on him. I couldn't find any blood in the wet dog hair.

He was breathing. I felt his chest rise and fall, and his heart was beating.

I then noticed his leather collar, the one he'd picked out himself at the pet supply store months ago. It was slashed, almost severed through at one point.

The Rysferatu had struck Fred at the time he was climbing up me. Fred had taken the sting intended for me, but his collar had provided him with protection from the venom. It may have been that blow that knocked him out, or when he hit the deck immediately afterward.

"Fred!" I cried. "Fred, buddy! Wake up, Fred!"

His eyes opened and he looked around, clearly not taking in his surroundings just yet, then I could see his vision clear and he looked up at me. He reached over and licked my hand, then closed his eyes again. Blood dripped on him from somewhere, but I couldn't tell where.

The light from the burning cargo ship seemed to start to strobe, then I realized we had company. Fire trucks and police cars were approaching. They blurred.

"Paco," I said. "Tell them U.S. Marshal Penny Ransome. Got that?"

"'Marsha Penny Randson?'"

"Close enough," I said, and my eyes closed and I didn't hear or see anything again for a while.

CHAPTER 71: WHAT HAPPENED

I awakened in a hospital bed to the sound of beeping and the quiet murmur of the business of hospitalization. Carts being pushed down corridors, visitors speaking quietly with patients, occasional bursts of laughter, and crying, and television shows, and someone asking for more pain medicine.

I closed my eyes and it all went away again.

When next I opened my eyes, U.S. Marshal Penny Ransome stood in the doorway, glaring at me.

"'Bout time you woke up, Carter!" she said.

"I'm in trouble again, aren't I?"

"I don't know where to begin," she said. "Piracy, murder, arson, kidnapping, child abuse, animal abuse, theft, explosives, the list goes on and on."

I smiled, weakly. "You forgot public mopery," I said.

"That's way down on the list," she said, then she returned my smile.

"How you doin', Carter?" she asked, coming into the room and sitting on a recliner positioned beside the bed.

I drew a deep breath and looked at the IV feeding unknown liquids into a vein in the back of my hand, and an oxygen sensor clamped to the end of a finger. Suddenly a cuff around my upper arm became tight as a machine automatically measured my blood pressure.

With my loose hand, I reached up and touched bandages wrapped around my forehead and skull.

"I guess I've been better. What happened?"

"'What happened'! That's what I've been waiting for you to wake up and tell me!"

"No, I mean, to me." I gestured at my head. "I don't remember this."

"Oh, that," she said. "The young man who was with you ..."

"Paco," I said, remembering him.

"Yes, Paco, he told us you were hit by something that fell from the sky, but you didn't seem to notice. It was like you were on autopilot, doing what needed to be done until you weren't needed anymore."

I shook my head, then winced at the pain. I could tell it was going to hurt for a while.

I told Penny what I could of my tour of the *Scrappy*, although we used the ship's real name. I left out some of the details, such as what supplies I carried and who had provided them to me, but most of my narration was truthful.

"There at the last in the hold, once it was bright enough to see, I felt kind of like the crew of the *Nostromo* in the movie *Alien*, as they walked among the pods containing the facehuggers. The place was full of egg sacs. The Rysferatu had been busy since boarding the ship."

Penny's face was grim. "That's why you blew up the ship."

"Not exactly. Blowing up the ship wasn't really my intent. It just happened that way."

"You should have called me," she said.

"I was thinking that the entire time I was on the ship," I said.

"Then why didn't you call me?"

I shook my head again, then stopped because it hurt too much. "I just wanted to be certain, and I kept getting in deeper and deeper. Next time, I promise."

"There won't be a next time," she said.

I agreed with her.

EPILOGUE

Fred was waiting for me outside the hospital when the nurse finally rolled me in a wheelchair to the exit. I'd been there for a week. It's a wonder the blow on my head hadn't killed me.

Julie was with him, grinning from ear to ear. She'd been taking care of him while I was incapacitated, but now that I was out, she was going to return to her cats. Our brief fling had been just that: A brief fling. But we remained friends. My family made a sizable donation to her zoo, providing grant money for continued research into the big cats, with a goal of finding a way to halt their path to extinction. Julie was named administrator.

My uncle the Senator was also waiting at the exit. He was the executor of my grandfather's estate, and it turned out my grandfather had not changed the will even though I'd turned government witness against my family and gone into hiding. With most of the others dead, I inherited nearly everything.

Any charges that might have been contemplated against me vanished, and didn't even make it to the attention of the working press. Research into the contents of the one egg sac recovered from under the dock at the abandoned industrial park had shown the value of the explosion that destroyed the ship and its contents. Prosecutors were advised they would be risking their own careers and good standing in the community if they attempted to bring any charge, at any level, against me.

I won't say who did the advising. I just knew someone, who knew someone.

Conspiracy theories, on the other hand, abounded. You may have seen some of them on YouTube. I found them amusing.

I don't know if there are any more Rysferatus out there. I imagine there must be, since the government got the one egg sac. If you should hear of a fearsome creature decimating any of America's enemies overseas, you might not want to dismiss it as mere fantasy or wish-fulfillment. And the chupacabra has been a monster in the dark for far longer than the Rysferatu ever existed.

Fred hasn't spoken to me or anyone since that night. I don't know whether it was the attack from the Rysferatu or the blow to the head he suffered when he fell to the deck after being struck. Maybe he feels like he's said enough for a while. Or perhaps he's decided that, if anyone were to figure out who I really am and come hunting us, it might be better for all concerned if he seems to be a normal, unspeaking dog.

He still gives me a look like he thinks he's smarter than me, from time to time, and I suspect the same thing. I'm glad he's still with me, even if he has gone silent.

I arranged for Paco and Rosalita to stay in the U.S., even though they entered the country illegally. They have family here, and I check in on them now and then.

Penny gained a promotion — I didn't have anything to do with it. Not directly, anyway.

And Fred and I still go for long walks, mostly for pleasure and exercise. At least, that's what I tell myself. So far, Fred hasn't sneezed, but there's always the next street, the next dark alley.

And if we find something, I'll call Penny. As soon as I've checked to see what it is, of course.

POSTSCRIPT

My name is Albert "Penny" Ransome. I am the U.S. Marshal that "Carter" refers to off and on in his story. As one may suspect from my name, I am not female, nor have I ever been female. That is just one of this man's efforts to throw the reader off his scent, so to speak.

Nor am I a short, black person. I'm 6-foot-3, I played football as a linebacker in college, on a scholarship, before I studied law.

As "Carter" hints at throughout his narrative, he is a professional liar, a skillful manipulator of facts and fancy in such a way that soon neither his victim nor anyone else — I dare say including "Carter" himself — knows what is true anymore.

The U.S. Constitution does not allow us to prevent this book from being published. Freedom of speech, and of the press.

However, I am authorized to categorically deny that there ever was a "Rysferatu." Nor is there a secret vessel as described in the pages of this book. And while "Carter" does have a dog, it does not speak and never has.

Similarly, there is no Financier as described herein. "Carter" did grow up in a crime family, but they were nowhere near as successful as he suggests in his story.

As for "Carter" himself, there are still charges he must answer for in federal court. Unfortunately, he has fled the country and is believed to be taking refuge in a small island nation where his family secreted away a small fortune.

If you encounter this man, do not confront him yourself, but call your nearest law enforcement agency.

(signed)
Albert "Penny" Ransome
Wilmington, Delaware

POST-POSTSCRIPT

Carter here. Also known as Wilson. I do not know who that "Albert 'Penny' Ransome" is, whose message was added to my story late in the pre-publication process. My dealings with the U.S. Marshals Service have always been with a diminutive African-American woman, not a white former linebacker.

Mostly everything I said in my story is true, although certain individuals and incidents have been altered somewhat to avoid embarrassment and potential lawsuits. And I might have exaggerated a few other details.

But the Rysferatu was real, and the government has an egg sac in its possession, somewhere, under deep, deep cover.

God help us all if whatever hatches gets loose!

REQUEST FROM THE AUTHOR

Now that the story has come to an end, what do you think?

Please take a moment to leave a review at the bookseller where you found it, even if it's just a few words. I will read your review and, if it's good, I might read it to Fred as well. He loves to hear from his fans!

And if you keep turning pages, you'll find the first chapter of our next adventure, cleverly titled *Help! Help! Cried the Dog*, due in stores soon if not already there.

DISCLAIMER TO KEEP THE LAWYERS HAPPY

This book is a work of fiction. Believe what you want, but if you think any of this is real, you are wildly mistaken and perhaps should consider seeing a therapist. If you see familiar names, places, events, organizations or anything else from daily life, or you think you see them suggested between the lines, know that they all stem from the writer's frenzied imagination and are not intended to be considered to be genuine in any way, shape or form.

Except for the dog. The dog is real.

This e-book is licensed for your personal enjoyment only and may not be re-sold or given away to other people. If you are reading this book and did not pay for it, or it was not purchased for your use only, then please consider buying your own copy. Thank you for respecting the hard work of this author, and remember: he needs to be able to afford to feed his dog, and only you can help. Tell all your friends, or buy copies for them as well!

AFTERWORD

Dogs don't talk. I (the real author of this tale) made that up. But the Scientific American has considered it: "Fact or Fiction: Dogs Can Talk," by Tina Adler, June 10, 2009. The URL to find it, as of the writing of this story, is https://www.scientificamerican.com/article/fact-or-fiction-dogs-can-talk/

Genetic engineering, as described in the story, is real, although the Rysferatu and how it came about is not. I hope! "Do-It-Yourself Genetic Engineering" by Jon Mooallem, Feb. 10. 2010, can be found in The New York Times Magazine. Here is the URL where I found it: http://www.nytimes.com/2010/02/14/magazine/14Biology-t.html

The Centers for Disease Control and Prevention (CDC) have a lot of valuable information about hantavirus, online at https://www.cdc.gov/hantavirus/

If you want to know more about ticks, here is an excellent site: http://www.tickinfo.com/

The female Longhorn Tick, by the way, is capable of reproducing without the need of a mate, and can have thousands of offspring.

And if you want to know more about carbon monoxide poisoning, I am happy to point you once again toward the CDC's website: https://www.cdc.gov/co/faqs.htm

I want to thank my early readers for their support and input, helping to make the story better: Robert, David and Chris, Holly, and Jack. All errors are mine, a result of reality being bent to make for a more exciting story. I hope you enjoyed it.

Glen Seeber
Midwest City, Oklahoma
September 2020

HELP! HELP! CRIED THE DOG: CHAPTER 1

A year had gone by since I last heard a sound from my dog, Fred. That isn't to say he didn't sneeze or scratch or bark or whimper or thump his tail against something, the way all dogs do. It's just that — well — we used to have conversations, Fred and me.

But that was before the ship with its horrifying cargo and the explosion that may have saved humanity but put me in the hospital for a week. Fred saved my life that day, but it cost him deeply, and me, too.

I'd grown accustomed to Fred's silence. A year will do that. A year can turn absence of something into a habit that you don't notice, except for those rare occasions when something happens that reminds you of the loss.

Which is why it came as such a surprise to me that day when Fred and I were taking a look at a house we'd acquired, sight unseen, out in the middle of nowhere in Kansas, and he suddenly backed down the stairs we'd been climbing, turned and looked me in the eyes, and clearly said, "No! Bad!"

Then he ran on down the stairs and out of sight. I heard the screen door we'd entered through bang, and I followed the sound outside to where I found him already inside the car. He had jumped in through the open passenger window, apparently in a great leap because I saw no scratch marks in the paint from his climbing up.

"Go! Go!" he said. "Now!" And he jumped into the driver's seat and started honking the horn.

I don't know what shocked me more, that after a year of silence Fred had finally found his voice again, or that there was something so off-putting about this house that he was frantic for us to get away from it.

I went out to the car, around to the driver's side, and Fred settled down, satisfied that I was there to make our escape from this nightmare house. But to his distress, I paused at the door, looking up at the house, wondering what had spooked him so.

The house was a rarity, a two-story Queen Anne structure, badly in need of paint and other maintenance, located miles from anywhere in the Flint Hills in eastern Kansas, nestled in a cut below a cliff that a century ago had served as a quarry. Its windows were intact, but shutters were loose, shingles were missing, and the porch had several floorboards that had succumbed to the elements over time.

I peered at the upstairs windows, wondering if a face would appear, staring back at me, or something else show itself that might signal the reason for Fred's reaction, but I saw nothing out of the norm. Just empty windows in an empty house on the empty prairie, backed up by the stone walls carved by men out of nature.

Fred honked the horn again, startling me.

"OK, Fred, I'm coming."

As I clambered into the car, Fred jumped to the passenger seat and nosed his way into the safety harness. I tightened the connections, then strapped myself in as well and started the car, pulling away from the house in a cloud of dry Kansas dust.

You might wonder why I, a human being, might allow myself to be ordered around by a dog this way. After all, dogs are just pets, right? They sleep and eat and poop and bark at strangers and sniff butts and play fetch and are "Man's best friend," only at the level of a possession or, in many cases, as a member of the family on, perhaps, the level of a 2- or 3-year-old.

That might describe the dogs you know, but then you don't know Fred.

I glanced over at him as I drove the narrow track away from the isolated house. He was looking back at me, but he wasn't smiling. His mouth was closed, tight, and he was shaking.

I hadn't seen him this wound up in a long time. Not since we'd fought the blood-sucking creature. He was the one who discovered it under the floor of the house we'd been given to hide in a little over a year ago.

"Fred? Are you OK, buddy?" I reached out to stroke his back and he growled, warning me off. Then he lay down in the seat and used his front paws to cover his face. Or, to be more specific, his eyes.

"OK, Fred," I said. "When you're ready."

The house was long out of sight in the rearview mirror by the time the rough and rutted track that pretended to be a narrow lane met the nearest highway, and I pulled out onto the blacktop and headed toward the nearest town with hotels that would accept pets. I wondered if we needed to visit a veterinarian while in town. This just wasn't like Fred.

Then again, Fred wasn't like any other dog. For one, Fred could talk — or until a year ago had talked — and had said so much more than the "Ai wuv oo" that you can find dogs "saying" in some YouTube videos. Fred had a vocabulary of hundreds of words, limited of course by the shape of his mouth, his tongue and palate. No surgery, no mad scientist experimentation, just careful, selective breeding with the intent of producing a super intelligent dog who could talk.

Fred was an anomaly, the only one of his litter who could talk. He was the runt of the litter and never achieved the full size of his siblings. And he was sterile, incapable of fathering any offspring that might carry on his ability to shape words that we humans could understand.

One might think he was a Jack Russell terrier, but he wasn't. He just resembled that breed, and may have had some of the breed in his DNA, but he also had poodle and lab and shepherd and collie and I don't know how many other kinds of dog in his family tree, all the way back to the original wolves from which all modern dogs are descended.

And after a year of silence, he had finally spoken again.

I was thrilled, excited even. But I was also scared and worried. To break a year's silence, to utter words of warning, to demand a hasty retreat, and to refuse a calming human touch, all added up to something really bad back at that house.

Or, as Fred used to say before losing his voice, "Bad! Bad!"

Until Fred was willing to communicate with me further about what had spooked him so badly back there, I needed to find out more about this house.

***

The second book in the Fred and Me series, *Help! Help! Cried the Dog,* should be available at the same bookseller where you found *Bad! Bad! Said the Dog.* A third book is also in the works, titled *Dead! Dead! Said the Dog.*

ABOUT THE AUTHOR

Glen Seeber studied how to write novels under best-selling author Jack M. Bickham at the University of Oklahoma then honed his writing skills working for newspapers for more than 40 years, since that was where a steady income could be assured. Now, as newspapers appear to be going the direction of the buggy whip, Glen has returned to his first love, the novel. He is currently writing another installment in the saga of Fred the talking dog. Follow him on Facebook at https://www.facebook.com/GlenSeeberAuthor or you can visit his personal website at https://www.glenseeber.com, and if you want to get in touch he can be reached at reader@glenseeber.com.

Don't miss out!

Visit the website below and you can sign up to receive emails whenever Glen Seeber publishes a new book. There's no charge and no obligation.

https://books2read.com/r/B-A-CKZL-JAQIB

BOOKS 2 READ

Connecting independent readers to independent writers.